Kopecki got off another wild shot and then he was crawling through the water on his hands and knees as they closed in on him. They dove on him, tearing and clawing and biting.

He felt their scabrous little hands brush his face. He hit at them, shot at them, blindly kicked out at them, but it was just no good. One of them buried its face in his throat and bit out a chunk of bloody meat in a red spray.

He screamed.

He made a gurgling sound.

Then he dropped the light. It was waterproof and floated in the rippling water, casting a weird glow over its surface that reflected up the walls. He swung and fought, but they kept clawing him until he was laid raw in a dozen locations. Then they climbed him like starving rats, biting and tearing as if they wanted to dig into him. He tried to fire off one last round, but he couldn't make it happen.

In the flickering flashlight beam, he saw why—his fingers were gone, chewed to nubs.

Then he saw the creatures. They were small, primeval things, naked, their flesh pallid and strangely mottled. They were albinos from living in the close darkness, spawning in it like cave rats. Their eyes were bulbous and white, mouths oval like those of sea lamprey, gums pink and set with crooked yellow teeth. Matted white hair hung from their scalps in twisting greasy braids like looping roundworms.

They made piping sounds as they fell on him, more coming out of the walls of the tunnel like burrowing worms.

Kopecki screamed as his blood turned the thrashing water pink around him.

He stared into their cruel, subhuman faces as they made to strike. This was the last thing he saw before they took his eyes, ripping them out by the cords of his optic nerves.

NIGHTCRAWLERS

TIM CURRAN

Copyright © 2014 by Tim Curran
ISBN 978-1-63789-626-6
Macabre Ink is an imprint of Crossroad Press Publishing
All rights reserved. No part of this book may be used or reproduced in any manner whatsoever without written permission except in the case of brief quotations embodied in critical articles and reviews
For information address Crossroad Press at 141 Brayden Dr., Hertford, NC 27944
www.crossroadpress.com

Cover art and design by David Dodd

First Crossroad Press Edition

1

The spades sinking into wet earth sounded like axes into soft necks. They rose and fell, shoveling out dirt and exposing roots, stones and worse things.

As the rain kept coming down, Kenney leaned under the overhang of the old farmhouse and watched the crime scene techs in their dark utilities and yellow rain slickers poking the earth, prodding it, digging into it like farmers working some grim harvest. He dragged off a cigarette and felt the chill and hated everything about it.

He thought: *Eight of 'em so far, eight goddamn bodies.*

They were laid out under plastic tarps next to the holes they'd been pulled from. Five women, two men, one child. So far. *So far.* Those two words kept ringing in his head. Eight bodies and here in a rural Wisconsin farmyard of all goddamn places. When he closed his eyes he saw their ravaged faces that sometimes weren't faces but discolored, fleshless canvases of bone. And that was all bad enough, mind you, until you factored in the condition of the bodies, the marks on them, and then it became considerably worse.

Chipney trod through the muck, said, "Eh, Chief, don't take it so hard. I was supposed to get married tomorrow. I had the week off. You think I'll get it now?"

"Not likely, Chip," Kenney said, blowing smoke into the wind. "Way things look, none of us are gonna be seeing any time off here."

Rain ran down the plastic bonnet of Chipney's hat, dripped off the tip of his nose. "Lieutenant... *Lou*, shit, I didn't see the bodies and I don't plan on it either. But, you know, people here are talking. They're saying things."

"What things?"

"You know, about the bodies."

Kenney flicked his cigarette away. It died in the rain like a shooting star. "What about 'em?"

"Well, that they're not...*whole*."

Kenney looked dire. "They're not."

"And that they look like they've been eaten."

Kenney felt bile bubble up his throat. "Chip, we'll discuss things later. For now, just get back out on that road. Keep an eye on those cops. Any goddamn newsies make it in here and I'll personally shove 'em up your ass."

"I think you might at that," he said.

It was a personal joke, and they both smiled.

Chipney stalked off into the rain, the night and wind.

The area was cordoned off. So far, nobody was really paying attention...but come morning?

The cops and techs raced around out there like spiders, backlit by flood lamps; the air reverberating with the diesel thrum of the generators.

Kenney stood there, thinking, thinking. Six hours before he'd been planning on a typical night—a takeout pizza and Monday Night Football—and then the phone rang. Wisconsin Electric had an easement from the county to run a new set of power lines to replace the old string that dated from the 1950s. This new run would cut right through a western fork of the Pigeon River State Forest outside Haymarket and continue across a stretch of abandoned farmland out on Bellac Road. Bellac was a lonesome stretch of abandoned fields, thickly wooded hollows, and gray ramshackle farmhouses and barns falling into themselves, all long abandoned. As the big dozer cleared a path through one particularly blighted field, the blade began to turn up bodies.

And that's when Kenney was dragged into it.

2

"Hey!" a voice called out. "We got another one over here!"

Kenney felt his heart drop into the swill pit of his stomach. Of course they did. Before this was over, God only knew how many there would be. Rain in his face, he started over there. The field was a hive of activity, and hour by hour the search perimeter was being widened. Fifty people here now. Seventy by tomorrow...and by next week? Kenney didn't want to speculate; it made his ulcers flare.

Rain fell down and cold mud sluiced and the crime scene was a misty, wet envelope of muck. Contact zones were staked and tarped with black plastic sheets. They snapped in the wind, the rain speckling them. Evidence techs were muttering amongst themselves and dropping tagged body parts into cold cans. Photographers were taking still pictures and videos of the carnage. Forensic specialists were collecting dirt and leaves and scraps of material that might have been clothing from the graves, sealing them in evidence bags. It was cold, wet, thankless work.

Kenney felt something like grease surge in his belly as he approached the young sheriff's deputy who'd sung out. He was one of about twenty state and local cops who were making a systematic grid search of the area for evidence. In a lateral line, , they walked and sank metal rods into the earth until they found a hole or depression.

Kenney got there quick as he could; wondering why the novelty of discovery hadn't worn off by now. Moving through that mire was like crossing quicksand. The ground sucked your feet in and if you hit a low spot, you'd go right up to your knee in the mud.

Spivak, the county pathologist, beat him to the scene.

Used to suicides and car accidents, Spivak was like a kid in a candy store. A small, sparse woman with auburn hair going gray at the roots and a pale face spattered with freckles, she looked outlandish in her rubber hip waders and black rain slicker.

When Kenney got there, she was carefully removing mud from a ribcage and pelvic girdle. Wearing plastic gloves, she worked meticulously, a tech assisting her. There was a dank smell in the air like rotting leaves.

"What do you got?" Kenney asked after she had been pawing about for five or ten minutes.

"Incomplete," she said. "No skull, missing vertebrae. I don't see an ulna here or a clavicle."

Kenney squatted down by her.

She held a grayed femur in her hands like a precious antiquity while the tech measured the zones. She rolled it over with her fingers. It was only partial, shattered at midline. Kenney could see the indentations in it like somebody had been working it with an awl.

"Teeth marks?" he said, before someone else did.

She nodded. "The smaller marks…could be rats. It's really hard to say. But these larger ones…well, I've never seen dentition like that before. Not animals in my experience."

"Human?" he said, a sickness rising in him.

She shrugged. "I don't know. Human teeth couldn't gouge like that, at least I don't think so."

Kenney didn't ask any more questions because he already had the answers. The marks were not from any animal she was familiar with. And she'd seen human bones gnawed and pawed by most predators and scavengers in the region—there was something about a human corpse they couldn't refuse.

Kenney wiped cold rain from his face. "People are gonna be asking questions," he said in a low, even voice. "Do you have anything? Even something preliminary?"

She gave him a blank stare, almost as if she was afraid to say what she was thinking.

Kenney sighed, staring off in the distance, at the cemetery crowning those low hills across Bellac Road, and thinking there were more bodies here than over there.

It was not a very comforting thought.

3

The fog held.

Stirred-up by the rain, it drifted in gaseous plumes and near phosphorescent blankets of white, moving through the fields and forests, spreading and encompassing. An hour after it started, it was thick and almost suffocating and nobody could see ten feet in any direction.

"You gotta love this soup," Deputy Riegan said, guiding the patrol car down a twisting, wooded lane, the headlights like glimmering white swords stabbing into the mist. "Can't see a thing."

In the passenger seat, Deputy Snow laughed. "Yeah, and we're supposed to keep the newsies and the nosy out. That's great."

Riegan moved the cruiser slowly, the front wheels dipping into puddles and potholes that made the whole car rock on its springs. The road wasn't much, just two dirt ruts with a barrier of unshorn grass between. So far, they had not seen a single newsie or nosy. They did, however, see three deer, several rabbits, and a large meandering porcupine. But that was the extent of it.

As Riegan drove, Snow stared out his rain-beaded window into the fog.

Below them was pastureland, mostly overgrown, the forest encroaching from all sides. Now and again, the fog would thin and he could peer down the grassy hill edging the road and see flooded fields, heaps of rocks, and a broken section of fence or two. There was little else out there.

"When I was a kid," Snow said, "we wouldn't come within a mile of this place."

Riegan, not a local, said, "Why?"

"I don't know. Spooks, I guess."

"Spooks?"

"Kid's stories, Dave. That's how it is out here. You get an abandoned farm and pretty soon kids are saying it's haunted. You know how it is."

"Sure."

Snow wanted to elaborate, but he didn't dare. He knew Riegan pretty well by this point, but there were some things you just didn't talk about with outsiders. Not without looking damn foolish or damn backward in your thinking. Riegan was not from Haymarket and he would never think like someone from Haymarket.

"It was like that growing up in Cleveland," Riegan said, as if he didn't care too much for the silence in the car. "Every neighborhood had a vacant house and every kid who lived nearby was sure it was haunted." He laughed. "Kids. That's all, kids."

"Yeah," Snow said.

He didn't believe that for a minute because he was a local and he had been tit-fed the local gossip since he was a child. It was a trivial part of his life, and his cop's hard-nosed practicality laughed it off, but it was still there, clinging to the underside of his mind. Especially when he woke from nightmares at three in the morning.

Don't you dare bring any of that up, he cautioned himself.

"Piss break," Riegan said, pulling the cruiser over.

"I could handle that. Goddamn coffee goes right through me."

They stepped out into the chill air and each found a bush to his liking and watered it. Snow had a hell of a time getting his flow to start because inside he was clenched tight as a fist. Though it was cool and damp, he felt warm. His scalp was prickling and his heart was pounding. It was all those childhood tales come back to haunt him. He knew they were all bullshit because they *had* to be bullshit, yet he couldn't get them out of his mind …especially not after dark.

"Damn that fog," he said. "Can barely see my dick."

"You couldn't see it anyway," Riegan told him and they both laughed, nervously, but they laughed. It felt good. For Snow, it was like fingers massaging the kinks out of his neck.

Riegan lit a cigarette. "Christ, I can't see doing this all night."

"No."

"Something bothering you, Rich?"

"No, I'm okay. Just tired."

"I hear you."

Snow watched the ground mist gathering around them. It was white and flowing like the steam from a pot. It had completely swallowed his legs beneath the knees and was draped in the trees like a garland. It made the dark forest beyond seem that much darker, that much more menacing.

Riegan chatted on about mundane subjects as he finished his cigarette—something that seemed to take forever—and Snow had the oddest sense that he was apprehensive, as if this place was somehow seeping into him, too.

"Hell was that?" he suddenly said.

"What?"

"Down there. Something moved down there."

Snow grabbed a flashlight from the cruiser and joined him at the side of the road. He clicked on the light, almost afraid of what he might see, and it reflected back at him. He played it around, a white beam spoking in the whiter mist, but there was nothing really to see. The hillside and its attendant grasses and wild growth descended into the soup. It was like a fog sea down there. Now and again, they caught sight of the shadowy forms of trees, but not much else.

"Probably a deer or something," Snow said.

"No. It was walking upright."

Snow felt a chill creeping up his lower belly. The fog subsided gradually and he could see the field down there, still misty and obscure, but visible. Riegan grabbed another flashlight out of the car and started down the hillside.

"Hey!" Snow said. "Christ, if that fog closes back in we won't find our way back to the road."

"So you stay there and call out to me."

Shit and shit. Snow did not like this. He watched Riegan go down the hillside, nearly slipping on the wet grass more than once and cussing under his breath. He made it to the bottom and waded out into the fog. He became indistinct and then disappeared completely.

Snow breathed in and out to calm himself.

After a few minutes of silence, he called out, "You okay down there?"

"Yes, mother!" came the reply.

Smartass. Now and again, Snow could see his light bobbing around down there, or he'd catch a quick glimpse of a shape moving behind it, but not much else. Shit. He took out his radio and let dispatch know they were out of the car and what their general location was. *In case they got to come looking for us.* He waited, pensively, his hand feeling oily on the barrel of the flashlight. *C'mon, c'mon, I'm about to have fucking kittens here.* The waiting was killing him.

Then—

"Hey!" Riegan's voice came floating out of the fog. "Get down here!"

"What?"

"Get down here!"

Shit, shit, shit.

Snow started down the hillside, watching his footing, his flashlight beam jumping about as he did so. The only good thing was that the fog appeared to be dissipating some, and he had no trouble tracking Riegan down. He was standing on a little grassy mound between two ancient black stumps.

"Well?"

Riegan scanned his light around. "There's somebody out here, Rich. Somebody real quiet."

Snow put his light out there. He saw only the mist, the weird dark shapes of heavy undergrowth and the boles of dozens of trees that seemed to have fallen against one another in a good windstorm, sometime in the past. For a second, he thought he saw a hazy shape duck behind one of them.

"There's nothing. Let's go. We should—"

"Shut up," Riegan said.

He panned his light around, turning on his heel in a perfect circle, trying to get a look at something. He was clearly listening and Snow listened with him. For what, he did not know. He was all for calling this off and getting back up to the cruiser. Enough of this Hardy Boys shit. If there was anyone out here— and God, how he hoped there wasn't—then there was no way in hell they were going to find them. They could have been hiding just about anywhere. And, hell, it was probably just a couple kids, anyway.

You know better than that. Kids around here would not come out here after dark. They all know better.

Riegan stopped.

There was a splashing off to their left. It could have been a bullfrog leaping into a pond for all they knew and it could have been something far worse. Riegan had his light over there. Snow heard a stick break over near the trees. Then another farther off into the fog. Another splashing noise followed by something like the quick drag of a foot through the underbrush or leaves.

He wasn't thinking it was kids now.

He was remembering all-too well what was said about this place.

Riegan came over. "Somebody watching us over by those trees," he whispered. "I'll sneak around behind them and flush them out."

"There's more than one," Snow said. "We better—"

"No, just wait. I'll flush him."

Before Snow could object anymore, Riegan darted off into the fog behind them. This was fucking bullshit. This wasn't deer season. This wasn't flushing game on a crisp November afternoon. This was…this was…

God, he just didn't know *what* this was.

Only that it was bad. So bad that it felt like his entire body was creeping, moving with the consistent hammering of his heart. Any moment now, Riegan was going to make contact with what was out there and he was either going to regret that or Snow himself would.

The fog seemed to be creeping in, moving in flowing white ghost sheets. Sticks cracked. There were splashing noises. Then something off to the left. The sound of someone walking through the muck in his direction with slopping, mucky sounds like a man in hip waders.

Snow pulled his gun, a Glock 9mm.

For godsake, don't shoot Riegan, whatever you do.

No, he wasn't going to do that. Whatever came out of the fog would not be Riegan. It would not even be human. It would be a dragging, hunched-over shape with a face like a rotten, blackening mushroom.

"Rich!" Riegan called out. "Do you see them? Jesus Christ, there's three or four of them...hey, do you see 'em?"

Snow was scanning the fog with his gun and flashlight now, just waiting, shaking and scared and he didn't know all what, but he was ready. He was ready to face whatever came out at him. He only hoped it would—

A scream tore through the night.

It was Riegan.

He ran toward the trees, and as the fog thickened around him he became disoriented. He wasn't sure where the hell he was, where Riegan was, and where the goddamn road was.

"DAVE!" he shouted. "DAVE!"

Riegan screamed again, only this time it was cut off like his throat had been slit or something had been stuffed in his mouth. Then there was silence. Not a single noise out there but the sound of raindrops falling from branches.

Nothing more.

Then splashing. Footsteps, slow and dragging, approaching from all directions. Snow saw an impossible, grotesque shape through the trees. Another darted off into the fog. He knew he should open fire or call for help, but inside he seized up. Nothing made sense.

Nothing but running.

He ran, stumbling and fighting until he reached the hill and then he was scrambling up it into the car. Once inside, he floored the accelerator, barely making the twists and turns of the road. Cold sweat poured down his face, and a choked whimpering came from deep in his throat.

He only knew one thing: Dave Riegan was dead.

4

In one of the trailers that had been set-up for the cops and techs to dry out in, Spivak said, "I've been doing this for fifteen years, Lou. I've seen it all. Maybe not as much as you, but I've had my share. I've only been in on a few murders and those have been pretty easy to peg—hunters gunned down, jealous husbands killing their wives. The usual. Around here, it's never anything spectacular."

"Until now?" Kenney said, sipping his coffee.

"Until now."

He could have told her all the things he'd seen, but he wasn't about to. He'd been a cop for twenty years now and he had the look of all seasoned cops—dead eyes, tight face, the grim demeanor. He supped full of the dark side of humanity on a regular basis and you could only swallow so much of that, hold so much of it down, before it changed you emotionally and physically. His job had cost him two marriages. There was always a price to pay.

"Those bodies...those remains," Spivak said, dread twisting beneath her words like worms considering bad meat, "there's no point in beating around the bush as to what we've got here. They were eaten and we both know it, we only don't know by *what*. The questions that plague me concern the bones...those teeth marks—at least what I think are teeth marks—I've never seen anything like it and I don't think you have either and, frankly, it's getting under my skin."

Of the bodies disinterred thus far, there was no observable evidence of death: fragmentation to the bone or trauma to the flesh that might have been caused by foul play. And he didn't like what that suggested at all.

He went to the window, looked out on the fields lit by flood lamps. He saw the collapsing hulk of the barn, the jutting finger of the silo, a few ancient outbuildings gone to kindling. Dark woods pressed in from all sides. The farm and its surrounding grounds—some eighty acres of tangled thickets, overgrown meadows, and swampy basins—was owned originally by a family named Ezren. Long dead now, the holdings were on paper with some relatives from out east. The farm had been vacant nearly thirty years.

Funny they haven't sold it off or broken it up into lots or something. The fields seem fertile, how come they haven't at least rented them out to other farmers?

Spivak stirred cream into her coffee. "I'm going to make some wild and possibly irrational assumptions here. The first few bodies were fresh. I'm gonna say they've been in the ground no more than six months. And what bothers me, really bothers me about them is that I can find no evidence of blood. No lividity, nothing. Some of the others, Jesus, I'm going to say—given the condition—that they died decades ago. Depending upon environmental factors, soil acidity, etc., it looks as if some of those bones are fifty, sixty years old. Maybe even older."

Kenney swallowed. "That old?"

"It looks like it."

Nightcrawlers

He, of course, had been thinking some serial crime here, mass murder. But if some cadavers were fairly fresh and others that aged, well that pretty much put the homicidal maniac theory to bed. He couldn't conceive of a killer whose activities spanned that stretch of time. It just wasn't feasible.

Spivak went on about dating bones, on rates of excarnation and dissolution. All things Kenney knew by heart, things he wasn't listening to now. Because beneath her authoritative, clinical demeanor, there was something else. Something trembling just beneath her words.

"Say it," he said. "Tell me the thing you're trying like all hell to avoid."

She stared out the window. "I told you how I found no traces of blood. I think the reason is that these bodies—some of them anyway—have been embalmed."

Kenney's face drooped, seemed to brush the floor. "What—"

But he never finished that for the door was thrown open and Chipney stood there in a spray of rain and wind. "Chief, we got a situation here. Seems we're missing one of our cops."

5

Out on the back forty, a tall, lanky deputy named Snow was going through it again while the fog crawled up from numerous hollows, playing around his legs like the family cat: "We...we were just, you know, keeping an eye on the area...policing it...making sure no reporters or curiosity seekers slipped through..."

Kenney walked up, surrounded by what seemed a battery of bobbing flashlight beams. The rain had subsided, but a wet, heavy mist hung in the air. He listened to Snow, though he had been pretty much briefed on what came down already. But he listened, and twenty years' worth of police work, of gut-sense, told him one thing and one thing only: this kid was scared. Terrified, maybe, like a little boy who'd just come face to face with the thing that lurked in his closet.

Kenney found a cigarette between his lips, had no memory of putting it there. One of the state cops gave him a light. "What's your name, son?" he said to the deputy.

"Snow, sir. Deputy Snow."

"That's not what your mother calls you."

There were a few forced giggles from the crowd of cops.

"Richard...Rich," he admitted, relaxing a bit.

Kenney led him away from the others, put an arm around him. "Okay, Rich. Tell me what happened. Just take it slow and tell me everything, best you remember. All right?"

Snow nodded. His eyes were glazed and fixed as if he were looking into some distant room. "Me and Dave…that's Deputy Riegan, sir…we were out here patrolling the road, making sure no one slipped through. You know how people are, sir…and this farm, Jesus, it's so big. Goes on forever."

Kenney dragged off his cigarette. "Sure. What happened then?"

Snow swallowed, letting the memory fill him up like poison. His face in the glow of the flashlight beams was yellow and rubbery, a stiff thing like a mask that was incapable of emotion. "We parked the cruiser on the road up there," he said, indicating the dirt road above them that cut through a crowded, dark thicket of Autumn-stripped oaks.

"Why did you decide to do that?"

"Well, sir, it's just…"

"It's okay, son. Just tell me the way it was."

Snow sighed. "Well, Dave pulled us to a stop because, you know, nature calls and all that. I joined him. About the time we were done, Dave said he saw something move down there…down *here*, I mean…and he went after it. He told me to wait with the car…"

Kenney listened. He was seeing it all in his mind. Riegan going down the hillside and out into the field, the fog moving in from all sides. Then he called Snow down to join him. He heard something or someone. Kenney knew Snow was telling him the truth, yet he had that gnawing feeling it wasn't *all* the truth. Something was unsaid here. Something was being carefully avoided.

"I started hearing it, too."

"What?"

Snow just shook his head. "I don't know...a splashing, mucky sound like someone was sneaking through the field, through the water. Dave went out there and tried to flush them out. I waited like he said. Then I heard him shouting for them to stop and I heard...I heard him say something, call out to me—"

"What did he say?"

Snow was trembling now, his fingers writhing at the sides of his uniform pants like snakes. His lips were pulled into a pencil-thin line. "He said, he said something like, *Rich, Christ, there's three or four of 'em out here. Do you see 'em?* I can't be sure. I couldn't see a thing, just hear something moving and then Dave screamed. I mean, he *screamed!*"

Kenney patted his shoulder. "Okay, take it easy."

"Sorry, sir."

"He didn't say *what* he saw, did he?"

"No."

"So you don't know if it was people or animals?"

"Not really. But if it was animals...well, if it was deer or something, he would have said. I'm sure he would have said so. With that damn fog, you just couldn't see anything."

"Just relax. We're gonna find him."

But Snow was shaking his head with such urgency it looked like it might fly off. "He *screamed*, sir...I heard him scream. Guys like Dave...like Deputy Riegan, they don't scream. He doesn't...didn't...he's not the kind that screams. Dave is brave, sir. Jesus Christ, he's my best friend."

"He panicked in the fog. It could happen to anyone."

"Bullshit," Snow said. "Guys like Dave Riegan do not scream, sir. Not unless...unless they run into something pretty goddamn bad."

Kenney talked him down, chilled him out. He'd been doing it for so many years to so many cops it was reflexive. The other men mumbled to each other about what Snow was saying, and Kenney told them to can it. Snow was starting to open up, really open up. Those unsaid things were about to be said. He was fighting back the sobs that bubbled in his throat, wanting out. The other cops stood around, feeling uneasy and awkward. They suddenly found the swampy ground and misting fields incredibly interesting. The silence was broken only by their boots in the mud, raindrops falling from tree limbs into the grass.

"What happened then?" Kenney said; his tone fatherly, almost a whisper. "Take your time."

Snow was breathing hard now. "I guess...I guess I freaked out. I went running around, shouting his name, but I couldn't find him. I don't know where he went or what he saw. I mean, I thought...I don't know for a second, I thought..."

"Tell me."

"It's crazy."

"Son, this whole business is crazy."

Snow drew in a lungful of air and then exhaled it like he didn't care for it much. "I thought I saw a...I don't know...a shape. Just for a second."

"A shape? What sort of shape? A man?"

Snow kept licking his lips. "Kind of...kind of like a man...but sort of hunched over, you know? His arms looked real long kind of...kind of like..."

"Like what?"

"Like an ape...real long and swinging."

"Oh, come on," someone said.

"Shut up," Kenney said. He pulled Snow still farther away from the others. He wanted to hear what he saw regardless of how *crazy* it sounded. It took some coaxing, but Snow told him again: it walked on two legs like a man, but hunched-over, weird, ape-like. Which *was* crazy, of course. Kenney was not sure what to read into that. Imagination? Hallucination? There were no goddamn apes in Wisconsin and he didn't believe in Bigfoot or any of that shit. Maybe it was a bear standing up. Hard to say. Fog had a way of distorting things, especially when you were panicking like Snow.

"I'm not sure what I saw, sir, I just don't know. Like I said, I freaked out. I lost my nerve. I guess then I got on the radio and called it in."

"You did right. We'll find him."

But Snow was still shaking his head. "You don't know this place, sir. You're not from around here. You don't know the things that happen out here."

Kenney motioned for one of the senior deputies to take him away. He needed some rest, maybe a stiff drink. As he was led away and up the hill to the cruiser on the road, Kenney just stood there, thinking about what he'd said. Thinking about it and not liking it one bit.

He looked over at Chipney. "Get everyone moving in a search pattern. Stay in visual contact. We don't need to lose anyone else in this goddamn soup." When the searchers were in motion, he turned to Hyder. "What's the kid talking about with that business? What's he mean, I don't know the things that happen around here?"

Hyder grinned foolishly like a drumming monkey, couldn't seem to stop. He licked his lips. "He's worked up, Lou. He don't know what he's saying."

"I think he does," Kenney maintained. "So let's have it."

Hyder managed to stop grinning. "Well, you know this is old farming country and all. But most of the farms, they're abandoned for years. It's a pretty desolate area. People make-up stories, you know how they are."

Kenney watched the man's face, took it all in — the little tic in the corner of his lips, the darting, nervous eyes. The way he seemed filled with a sudden need to get away like a little kid with a full bladder.

Kenney lit another cigarette off the butt of the last. "No, I don't know how they are. Maybe you should tell me."

"Well, all these woods and empty fields, Lou. They play on the imagination. And those farmhouses, falling down with rot and neglect—"

"Are you saying this place is haunted?"

Hyder laughed uneasily. "No, not haunted exactly. Bellac Road, you know, people wouldn't live out here. Said they heard things, saw things. Weird things. Just a bunch of bullshit, Lou. You give these backwoods types some empty land and soon enough they're talking spooks."

Kenney was going to push it a little farther, get to the root of it all—because there had to be one, and, who could say, maybe in some offhand way it would contribute to the investigation—but Chipney came splashing through the mud, leaves festooned to his pants and boots.

"Lieutenant, come and take a look at this."

Kenney tossed his cigarette and followed him out deeper into the field. The rain had turned the land into a sluicing river of slush. The fog parted at his approach. The search party was paused before a wide, smooth stone about the size of an ottoman. On it there was a muddy footprint.

Kenney got in real close so he could see it under the wash of the flashlights.

It was a human footprint…or nearly. The print of a bare foot, but broad, splayed out. But maybe it was just the splattered mud that gave it such an abnormal appearance.

He looked up at Hyder. "Who in the Christ would be running around out here barefoot?"

But Hyder just shook his head, pressing his lips tight as if maybe he was afraid he might accidentally say something. Something he just did not want to admit to.

6

There were ten of them, moving through the wet darkness, the beams of their flashlights cutting through the murk, like swords. They moved in a lateral line, one arm's length apart. The country was filled with tall, unshorn grasses and craggy bushes, low swampy dips filled with leave-covered pools and cast-off branches.

"You wanna be careful where you step out here, boys," Hyder was saying. "This country can be treacherous. We get a lot of rain like this on top of that clay, sinkholes develop...can suck a man down five, ten feet before he knows what's what."

"Just keep your eyes open," Kenney said, something unpleasant beginning to worm in him now.

Hyder's eyes were wide in his rain-misted face. "Yeah...strange things happen out this way...a funny place. Always has been. Air's just funny, maybe, got a...a...negative charge to it, I guess."

Kenney stopped suddenly, unsure.

"What's the matter, Chief?" Chipney asked.

"Nothing," he said. "Nothing at all."

They kept going. No one was saying a thing. The only sounds were those of boots being pressed into the mud, withdrawn. Kenney placed each foot carefully, half-expecting to trip over a log or twist his ankle in a hole. Ten minutes into it, he started getting real good at it. He didn't have to think about where he was walking or what he might be stepping on, because his feet were on auto-pilot and they seemed to know. Instinct, maybe.

The forest began to press in closer from all sides. It was black and wet and craggy, the wind making the high branches rattle together like bones. Squat, gnarled bushes formed themselves into unnatural shapes that stood high as a man and broke up the grid search. More than once, Kenney thought the bushes moved out of the corner of his eye, and he was struck by a mad, irrational idea that they were alive and sentient. Moving, erasing the search party's footprints, turning everyone around and shuffling them like cards so they would never find their way out again.

Crazy thinking, sure, but he wasn't blaming himself for how he felt or how the others felt, the way their faces were drawn and tight like the skulls beneath were trying to work themselves free. This place got to a man, and try as you might, you could not put a finger on it. But it was there. In your guts and head, crawling up the back of your spine. Maybe Hyder was right: maybe it *was* the air. Maybe there was something negative about it, as unscientific as all that was.

I better pull it together here. I can't let these boys see that I'm scared shitless. But I am. I really am and I honestly don't know why.

It was like the skin of the known universe had been peeled back and he was looking over its rim, knowing there was something out there in that fathomless blackness that would drive him mad if he saw it.

He figured if he had been alone out there, he would have run screaming into the night.

Again, it made no sense, but it was there, twisting inside him with a bleak sense of expectancy.

Some of the men were getting apprehensive, too. They began to speak in nervous whispers to break the silence. One man hummed to himself. And Hyder, damn fool bastard, he kept running his mouth like a machine with no off switch. Talking about how livestock would sometimes stray out towards Bellac Road and you'd never see them again, except maybe bones that would show up in a dry wash come July.

He was afraid and Kenney knew it, but he still had little sympathy for the guy.

He was the undersheriff, and according to state law, the second highest-ranking law enforcement officer in the county, a leader of men. And here he was talking spook stories and getting the troopers and deputies worked up. Kenney had an urge to punch him right in the mouth.

But that was stress talking.

Stress had a way of rising up, getting big and bloated and angry, looking for something to vent itself on.

And the stress was bad out here. The damp, the mist, the chill breath of night air. The darkness moving around them. Kenney felt it just like the others. He kept seeing shapes slinking around them, hearing muted sounds like maybe someone or something was trying real hard *not* to be heard. And it all got to him, laid down low in the pit of his belly in a buzzing, almost electrical mass of terror.

The mist had become a fog that was oozing out of the earth like plumes of smoke. It was thick and twisting, faintly luminous. The bobbing flashlight beams seemed to reflect off it, filling it with surreal moonlike phosphorescence. It climbed their legs and rose higher and higher, blotting out the landscape like a shifting, ominous sheet.

The men had stopped moving. Something was building, and they all knew it deep inside. It made the hairs stand-up on the back of Kenney's neck, made his flesh go clammy and tight. His eyes were wide and unblinking, his voice locked down tight in a flow of black ice.

Hyder, his voice high and girlish, started to say, "Was…was a fellah had a farm just south of here and things…things started happening…something got to his cows—"

"Quiet," Kenney said. The air was hot and cold around him, suddenly filled with life, with stealthy motion.

Hyder made a moaning sound low in his throat.

In the treeline off to their left there was noise, motion, activity. Underbrush crackled and sticks snapped and there was a weird rustling sound like a tree being shaken. Everyone was still and tense.

Kenney felt sweat trickle down his forehead, heard a humming in his ears which he knew was the frantic rushing of his own blood. The noises seemed to be all around them now— slopping, dragging sounds. Moving closer, moving away, circling them like a noose. Any moment now, it was going to reveal itself.

He could smell a foul odor like rotting vegetables in a root cellar. A thick and pungent closed-up smell. The stink of damp, secret places and noisome decay.

"Funny sounds," Hyder said under his breath. "Always funny sounds out here."

Kenney gave him a look, and he shut up. Thankfully. This was all enough without that idiot whistling past the graveyard.

"Chief…sounds like they're all around us," Chipney said.

"That's because they are."

No wonder Snow had been ready to come out of his skin. It was terrible out here. There was something positively unnatural about this place. But if someone were to ask him what, he couldn't have told them. The sounds of movement were everywhere…squishing noises, feet stepping through mud and splashing through puddles.

He did not think it was other men. And not animals either. What had Snow said? *Kind of like a man…but sort of hunched over.* Something hunched over with long arms like an ape.

Jesus, this was insane.

His ears began to pick up other noises, and he wondered if he hadn't been hearing them the entire time. He couldn't put a finger on it at first, but as it rose up around them, yes, then he knew. *Breathing*. A wet, congested breathing like a man sucking wind through a mouthful of rotting leaves. And there were other things, too: shrill, echoing sounds, high and weird whispering.

And then, gradually, everything faded into the night, the mist, and there were just the ten of them, silent as monuments, waiting and waiting. There was nothing else to hear. Just rain dropping from the trees. The breeze. The sound of their own heartbeats. The creaking of leather Sam Browne belts.

"Wasn't nothing," Hyder said, enormously relieved. "Wasn't nothing but our own noises turned back on us. Things get funny out here. Fog'll do it. Sure enough. I was out deer hunting once and I swore something big was stalking me through the woods. But it was just my own sounds. That's all it was."

Nobody was buying any of that, but the less said the better.

They moved on and kept tight to one another, navigating around hedgerows and thickets and boggy hollows that threatened to swallow them whole. Nobody was saying much and Kenney knew that one word, just one word from him, and the lot of them would head back and call it a night. But that wasn't going to happen. Not until he knew what was going on out here.

Scraped by branches and twigs, soaked right up to his knees, he began to see what looked like ancient foundations set in the ground. He saw a wall off to the left built atop a sloping hill, but just a suggestion of it jutting from the earth like rotting teeth. The shattered remains of a tower or silo. A series of cracked, frost-heaved slabs rising from the earth. Grassy mounds like inverted bowls looming around them, things which could not be natural.

"What is this place?" he asked Hyder.

Hyder kept swallowing, his Adam's apple bobbing up and down like there was a hardboiled egg stuck in there. "Was a town here…long time ago," was all he said.

Kenney saw a vine-covered wall of limestone block set into a hillside, the dark and near-collapsed mouth of a doorway set into it. Off in the woods, there were other shapes, hunched and broken.

The foundations became more numerous. Some had elms growing up from their cellars. Others were like seed pots that wild, reaching knots of leafage sprouted from. They stopped before one that reached for hundreds of feet like the skeleton of some Colonial blockhouse. They could still make out a worn set of steps leading down into a blackened, flooded cellar. They played their lights over the leaf-clotted surface and Kenney thought for one lunatic moment he saw some yellowed face peering up at them from just beneath the oily, turgid pool.

But then it was gone.

Somebody kicked a stone in and it sank without a trace.

Chipney and a couple others walked along the ledge, putting their lights onto something in the distance like a circle of tombstones rising from the earth. Hunched and broken, they were gray with age and threaded with lichen and mold, ground-fog trembling at their bases.

"Christ sake," Chipney said. "What sort of place was this?"

Hyder said, "We should turn back. No way Riegen made it out this far…not out here."

"Maybe he did," Kenney said. "If he got lost in that fog, he might have seen this place, came in for shelter."

But that got a morose chuckle from Hyder. "No, no way. He wouldn't come here. Not here."

"He might," one of the cops said. "He's not local."

Kenney paused there, lighting a cigarette. "Meaning?"

Hyder just shrugged. "Locals know better than to come out here. Nobody comes out here."

"Why?"

"What reason could they have? Easy to get lost. These old ruins are dangerous, real dangerous. I advise against going any farther. We better wait until morning. That's the sensible thing to do."

Kenney could feel that the others, even his own men, were in perfect agreement. He sympathized with them because he didn't like this goddamn place any more than they did, but a cop was missing. The longer he went missing, the worse the chances were of him being found. Kenney didn't know Riegan, but he was willing to bet he had a family. Would they understand the search being called off because…because men were getting the fucking willies in the fog?

Pretty damn sure they wouldn't.

"You'd leave one of your own out here?" he said to Hyder.

"Well, no, but…"

"What if it was you, Undersheriff? Would you like to spend the night out here by yourself?"

"No…not out here. Not out here."

The more Kenney learned about Hyder, the less he liked the man. Superstitious, afraid of his own goddamn shadow…he wasn't much of a man and even less of a cop. Besides, maybe Kenney didn't know all the crazy, pumped-up old wives' tales about this damnable place—and he was beginning to suspect there were more than a few—but, spooks or no spooks, if a man got lost and he saw some ruins he could duck into, he was going to do it. What Kenney wanted to do was give Hyder a good going over, get to the facts that had him and the local cops shit-scared of this place. But there just wasn't time. He kept thinking of what was out there in the fog…he knew it was bad, but he wasn't about to buy any of this nonsense about spooks.

Chipney and some of the other men were looking through the wreckage, flashlight beams scanning leaning doorways and collapsed sod roofs, disintegrating walls and cobbled walks disturbed by black tree roots. Everywhere, hooded shadows crept and crawled. Empty windows were filled with a leering, distorted blackness.

Kenney was wondering how long the place had been vacant.

Centuries, occurred to him, but was that possible?

He supposed it was. Wisconsin had been settled a long time. The British had forts there in the 17th century, and towns always sprouted up around those forts. Maybe this was the remains of one of those places.

He and Hyder threaded through an ancient cemetery of leaning, ivied headstones and moss-encrusted slabs, all weathered unreadable. Markers were swallowed by weedy tentacles. Grotesque, dead and decayed oaks sprawled morbidly over rows of crumbling tombstones that crowned blighted hillsides and sank from view into hollows of choked briers.

Kenney didn't like the smell of the place.

It would have been normal to smell age and time here, to smell decay and rot. But what he smelled was far worse—a palpable, vaporous stench of contamination. He felt…he wasn't sure, but something like an ominous presence, a great anxiety that made him either want to turn and run or just sit down and give up. It made no sense. It ate the heart out of him.

"We should go," Hyder said, his voice high and helpless.

But Kenney shook his head. "Not yet…there's something here…something…"

"Then you feel it, too?"

"Yes."

Kenney in the lead, they moved off deeper into the mummy of the village, through weedy thoroughfares, up deserted hillocks and down into small vales where charnel shadows bled from the diseased earth like black blood. Their lights illuminated odd, twisted shapes in the rank grasses, but no one dared look too closely. Atop a steep grade, ringed in by denuded oaks, they found the remains of a moldering house of gray, nitrous stone covered in a knotted profusion of withered creepers.

"Let's have a look," Kenney said to Hyder, telling the others to wait outside.

Hyder stared unblinking at the jackstraw tumble before them, looked upon it like it were some hollowed skull whispering secrets and shook his head. "I'd rather not," he said, his voice dry as cinders in an ashpot. "I don't like any of this and I don't mind admitting it."

"Well, I'm going in," Kenney told him. "You stay out here, look around and see if you can find your balls—"

Hyder grabbed him by the arm and whirled him around. He was surprisingly strong. "Now, you listen to me, Mister Fucking Hotshot Detective. You ain't from these parts and you don't know dog turds from diamonds. Riegan ain't goddamn well here. You wanna start searching again in the morning, fine, but right now let's get our asses out while we still can."

Kenney yanked his arm free. "I don't know what kind of kiddie spookshow game you're playing here, Hyder, but I've had it right up to here. Now start acting like a cop or get the hell out of my sight. I've had it with you."

"Goddammit, Kenney, don't be a fool. We're in danger here. Real danger."

Kenney shoved him aside and ducked through the low doorway. Inside it was like an oppressive envelope of contagion and degeneration. Flashlight held before him, he clambered over the debris of fallen walls, pushed on through dust and countless seasons of dead leaves. Above him, wan moonlight spilled in through the latticed timbers overhead. He found himself on a slanting floor of fissured flagstones that continued on for maybe thirty feet, before falling away completely into a cellar of heaped rubble, black water, and jutting shapes.

He heard Hyder coming in behind him as he knew he would.

"Look at this," Kenney said, shining his light down into the inundated pit.

A jawless skull broke the surface of the stagnant pool, wet leaves plastered to its cranium. The slats of a ribcage, a pelvic girdle. Dozens of bones.

"Like some litter pile," he said.

Hyder turned away, refusing to discuss it.

Kenney lit another cigarette. His fingers trembled as he held the lighter to the end and blew out smoke. His nerves were shot. But he didn't want Hyder to know that. He didn't want him to think for a moment that he was a superstitious idiot like him.

"So this place is supposed to be haunted, is it?"

Hyder sighed. "I didn't say that exactly, now did I?"

"Funny, though. Place like this…should be a natural magnet to kids. But I haven't seen any graffiti, beer cans. Nothing. How do you explain that?"

"Those that know of this place know better than to come here. That's all I'm saying."

"Listen to you. And in this day and age."

"I call it common sense."

Kenney blew smoke into the dank night. "But what do they say exactly? People around here, what do they say?"

Hyder, his face bloodless in the glow of the flashlight beams, said, "When I was a kid, during the daytime, sometimes on a dare we'd come out here. Maybe take a brick home as proof you were here. Something like that. This place has always been bad…people hear things out here, see things."

"Ghosts?"

"No…not ghosts. Not exactly."

Kenney was examining the wall near what might have been a hearth. He could see things scratched into the stone, weird symbols of some sort. They didn't appear to be letters, at least none that he had seen before. There were other things, too, but they were obliterated by innumerable seasons of rain and snow and sunshine. But what really interested him were the marks dug across the fields of etchings—deep ruts like the tines of a garden trowel had been dragged across them.

Kenney traced his fingers through them. "What do you make of this?"

Hyder shook his head. "Please," he said, his face beaded with sweat. "Let's go, let's just go."

Kenney decided it was time.

It took them about five minutes to get free of the village. Another five before the black forest blotted it from view. And the entire time he was thinking that something horrible had happened to that shuttered ruin, something horrible that was still happening. The place had gone bad, been poisoned to its very roots. The marrow of the village was rancid and contaminated, its blood gone black and toxic like bile. And a man could puff out his chest and pretend he didn't feel it, but it was there. An abominable physical presence.

Aware, alive, and deadly.

7

As they walked back down into the foggy, damp lowlands and the mud sluiced around them and the shriveled, denuded bushes rose up and beckoned like misshapen skeletons, no one spoke. They stayed close to one another and looked at each other, neither smiling nor frowning. Just glad to know they were not alone. To a man they wondered how they would explain any of this the next day in the bright sunlight, how they could possibly justify what it was they'd felt this night when instinctual dread and childhood terror were displaced by reason and logic.

They kept going, and the mist held them in a terrible alchemy of dancing phantoms. The world was filled with strange, unseen forms and secret rustling noises that stopped whenever they dared look.

Kenney was sweating now despite the wet chill.

He could feel perspiration running down his spine, beading his forehead. His palms were greasy. He kept hearing sounds— off to the left, then the right, then directly in front of them, behind them. It was maddening. When he stopped to listen, everything went silent as the grave.

He was expecting to see something at any moment. Something grim loping out of the shadows at them.

Hyder was talking again, telling everyone it was just a deer. Some big buck rooting out there in the bog lands. Nothing more, nothing to be worried about. But it was obvious from his voice that he was trying to convince himself of this…and failing.

Kenney thought he caught sight of some vague form ahead bleeding into the night, but then it was gone.

One of the sheriff's deputies said, "*Christ, did you see that? What the hell was that?*"

And Hyder started to answer, then he closed his mouth as something came at them out of the polluted, ectoplasmic mist…a sound.

Whispering.

Not just one or two disembodied voices like before, but dozens, maybe hundreds of voices whispering and whispering, competing against one another. That wall of eerie sibilance rose and fell, echoed through the night like some sibilant harmony. You could hear individual voices in there, but never identify what it was being said.

Kenney and the others stopped moving. You could hear someone breathing, someone making a strangled sobbing sound, someone else chattering their teeth. Kenney was filled with concrete. At any moment he would fall through the moist crust of the earth, plunge into some dark abyss like a sinking ocean liner.

The whispering faded as if maybe it was coming from some far-distant quarter and then came right back at them again like a boomerang, a malevolent and baneful noise of countless whispering voices. So loud now, so in-their-face godawful, it seemed it was being run through an amplifier.

"What the hell is this?" Chipney demanded.

The men started moving in circles, weapons drawn. Unsure, afraid, terrified even. They were muttering to themselves and one man was reciting the Rosary. Discipline was unraveling like a ball of yarn and they were bumping into each other and stumbling through the sea of cold mud, trying to stay together, but wandering off.

Kenney was feeling it, too. The flesh at his balls was creeping.

"Stay together!" Hyder called out in a weak, horrified voice. "We…we gotta stick together and march out in a line. Don't you see? Anything comes at us, we shoot it, we shoot it down for chrissake—"

"Quiet!" Kenney snapped. "Shut your goddamn mouth!"

He heard it as before: a stealthy, sentient motion out there that stopped as they stopped, took advantage of the noise of the search party walking through the muck to get in closer. But now it was no longer bothering to disguise itself. It was coming for them.

The mud seemed deep as quicksand now and the fog grew thicker. It swirled around them, covered them, moved in a phantasmal and cloistral mist, enclosing them in a shroud of dampness. The men stumbled through it, tried to find their bearings, but were gradually separating in their confusion.

And Kenney knew it, but was powerless to do anything about it.

He called out, trying to rally the men, but no voice could still the confusion and terror that ate away their unity. And that was the worst possible thing—no command, no discipline, no unit integrity, everything steadily going right to shit until there weren't ten men in those saturated fields, but ten little boys, lost and scared and confused.

Somebody screamed and Kenney saw one of the deputies—Kopecky, he thought—waist-deep in a sinkhole, struggling like a mastodon in a tar pit. He flailed and writhed and that only fed him deeper into the throat of the hole. A few of the cops staggered away so they wouldn't get drawn down, too, but the others tried to reach him and were soon up to their calves in the muck.

Kenney made a try himself, one leg sinking up to the knee in the swampy filth.

The sound of footsteps moving at them through the mist was closer. They would strike now that the searchers were mired in the mud, trapped and hobbled and most certainly stuck like struggling insects on a fly-strip.

Jesus, I can feel it. It's about to happen.

The whisperings were all around them. Loathsome, hunched shapes flitted through the mist with amazing speed and agility. They squealed and grunted like wild boars.

Kopecky was up to his chest in the awful mire and his face was wet and spattered with grime. As everyone watched, a pair of grotesque white hands came up from the oozing muck, the fingers bonelessly wrapping around his throat like the tentacles of some bathypelagic horror, and he was drawn down and was gone, a few turgid bubbles rising up. And happened so fast, no one could be sure if those spongy, bleached things were even hands at all.

And that was it.

Everyone lost it.

8

When Kopecky opened his eyes, he was alone in the mud and the darkness. He tried to think, tried to put it together. They were moving through that field and then…and then those shapes came out of the fog. Not human shapes at all. No, debased, degenerate, grotesque. They he went down the hole.

You didn't go down, you were pulled down.

That's when panic hit.

He tried to scramble to his feet, but the mud was slippery like some semi-gelatin ooze. It smelled like corpse slime. A yellow and aged stench that crawled down his throat and settled in his gut. He managed to rise finally and immediately bumped his head on the earthen roof of the passage. A jutting root nearly tore his ear off.

He was in a tunnel.

A subterranean crawlspace made for dwarves or troglodytes. Frantically he felt at his belt. Yes, he still had his gun but his radio was gone. Not that it would have done him much good down in this stygian hole, anyway. He fumbled around on his belt until he found his little penlight. He thanked

God he carried it now. He also thanked God that he was not overly claustrophobic.

It was practically blinding in the blackness.

Above, a little light like that would have illuminated five or six feet, but down there it was like a searchlight. Such was the quality of the darkness.

He panned the light over the muddy floor. He could see what looked like a drag mark fading into the distance. He must have been knocked unconscious when he fell. Yes, that had to have been it. Then he pulled himself this far by sheer instinct alone, not really awake, just scratching his way forward like a mole.

He would simply go back that way and get out.

That's it.

That's all there was to it.

He began moving back down the passage, trying real hard not to think of what the tunnel was for or who had dug it. It wasn't a good idea to be thinking about things like that. The tunnel seemed to be arching steadily towards the right at a gentle angle. There wasn't much to see—tree roots spoking down, mud, and standing water.

But dry. Oh hell, yes, drier than dry. Like I've been inhaling bone dust and ashy cremains.

The passage began to widen, and he felt hopeful.

I'm going to get out of this shit. Just you watch and see.

It was optimism that he figured was neither unrealistic nor misplaced. A good state of mind was more important than anything now. If he could keep his spirits bolstered, his mind would react in kind and find a way out. If he let despair overtake him, he would panic and go mad scrabbling in the muck and darkness. That was unacceptable. He had a wife and son. He needed to get back to them. Besides, the others would be moving heaven and earth to find him. But they couldn't do it alone; they needed his help.

He moved on, duck-walking down the tunnel.

Now and again, he would pause and listen. He wasn't sure what for, but it seemed necessary. In the back of his mind he told himself that it was for the sound of his rescuers. Maybe it was, partly. But the dark truth was that he had grown up in Haymarket and he knew the stories like everyone did. Insane things about the underground network of passages and, worse, who had tunneled them out.

Now that the passage was wider and taller, he moved forward in a hunched-over crouch. The water had deepened some, up over the toes of his boots now, but it did not alarm him. This is the direction he had come from and this was the one that would get him back out.

Wait until he told people he had been down beneath—

Shit.

He shined the light around and there was no mistaking what he was seeing. There were skeletons protruding from the bowed red clay walls, five or six of them still articulated by the dried mud itself. They looked like they were trying to crawl free, and for a moment, as his heart seized in his chest, that's exactly what he thought they were doing.

But no, they were long dead.

Yellowed and pitted, crumbling from age. They had been down here a long time and looked oddly like withered corn shocks as he caught them out of the corner of his eye. Alarmed, he fought back the panic that rose inside him like bile.

You don't have time for fear. You panic now and you'll look just like them after a month down in this goddamn hole.

He moved on.

With a sinking feeling in his gut, he realized that the passage was gradually canting downwards. It would take him deeper into the black bowels of the earth and the realization of this ignited a primal dread inside him. His skin pulled tight, his face and neck felt prickly. He waited there, unsure what to do now. The light trembled in his hand. Water dripped from above and ran down his face like tears. He began to feel the effects of confinement, of gnawing claustrophobia. The walls seemed to be pressing in on him. For just one sweaty second there, he thought he saw them moving.

He edged his way farther down the passage.

Jesus, it just kept going down and down. Its cant was gradual, but the farther he went, the higher the brown slopping water rose until it was nearly up to his knees. But just ahead, the light showed him that it opened up again. He would go that far before turning back. He would see what there was to see...even if it was just more old bones.

You're doing okay, he told himself. *Just keep your nerve.*

He relaxed a bit. He couldn't let imagination master him. He had his light, he had his gun. The walls were not closing in on him and the air was just fine. The very fact that there *was* air was proof positive that this network connected with the surface somewhere.

He barely even smelled the gaseous stink now.

After awhile, he figured, you could get used to just about anything.

He made himself move on until he was in a chamber that was tall enough to stand in. The water was up above his knees by then and steadily rising. It dripped like rain from above.

He moved on.

The tunnel was narrowing again, the floor dropping away much faster. He kept at it until the water was up to his thighs. He didn't like that. He saw no sign of light ahead, as from an opening to the surface, just a heavy weave of darkness that was black and sewer-smelling. The passage opened up, but only into a pool of murky water that looked deep.

No way in hell he was going down there.

Time to backtrack.

He put the light back the way he had come. Yes, it was more reassuring to go in that direction. At least the tunnel canted gradually higher and he would be out of the water. He figured he couldn't have been too far under the surface. Worst came to worst, he was going to dig his way out like a rat.

Behind him, splashing.

A bolt of white fear exploding in his belly, he turned around quick. For just the briefest of seconds, the light reflected off what looked like dozens of shining white eyes. He nearly dropped the light, a small, strangled cry breaking in his throat. When he got control of it, he put the beam back down there.

Nothing.

Just that dark pool of filthy water. A few ripples played over its surface and he did not want to know what was causing them. He turned and started up. He made it maybe ten feet when he heard the splashing echoing up from the pool again and his flesh went tight. He put the light back there and saw nothing.

It's your nerves, it's just your goddamn nerves.

He breathed in and out and turned back…and cried out.

Movement.

Just a hint of it. As he brought the light back around, he saw a dark elfin shape scurry past. In his mind, he had a distorted image of something like a hunched over black cat walking upright, front paws dangling from chest-level.

He put the light around in trembling arcs, but there was nothing there. Still, he took no chances. Kopecky was a cop with a cop's sense of reality. He didn't believe in boogeymen, but he *had* been raised on the local superstitions and spook stories. His cop's gut sense told him to err on the side of caution and he pulled the Colt 9mm from its holster.

He moved on, the passage narrowing.

The clay walls pressed in, the roof angled downwards. Water dripped on his head, making his scalp feel sodden and oily. Tree roots reached down like dead fingers. One brushed the back of his neck and he nearly cried out. He moved the light around, scanning it back and forth. And as he did so, he saw something that *did* make him shriek.

A face.

Again, he saw it for no more than a second, but it was definitely a face, white and grinning, looking oddly swollen as if from insect bites. Its eyes bulged from their sockets like white eggs, huge and sightless.

Automatically, he jerked the trigger of the Colt and sent two rounds. Whether he hit it or not, he did not know. He moved the light around and it was gone. It was not in front of him or behind him. It had just disappeared like a ghost.

He sensed movement again.

Panicking, he shined the light in every direction, looking for a target, anything to take out his fear on. He heard more splashing from the pool farther down the passage. He caught a momentary glimpse of something in the light like a huge white spider skittering away. He fired. Something brushed the back of his neck. He turned and fired.

They were all around him and he knew it.

But they were so fast, so well adapted to their environment that he never stood a chance against them. He fired twice more at leaping shadows. A white hand came at him like a blur out of the darkness. Before he could even get the gun up, gray gnarled talons laid his cheek open. The skin hung open in a flap.

He needed room to fight, but the tunnel was confined and claustrophobic.

Another one of them came at him, but this time he heard it and brought the butt of the gun down on its head before it reached him. It made a squealing sound and vanished. Its head was soft like the bell of an inky cap mushroom.

Kopecki got off another wild shot and then he was crawling through the water on his hands and knees as they closed in on him. If he could just make it to the place where he found the skeletons, he would have room to fight. But they weren't going to allow that because he was much bigger than them. His size and strength made him dangerous on open ground where he could use these things to his advantage.

They dove on him, tearing and clawing and biting.

He felt their scabrous little hands brush his face. He hit at them, shot at them, blindly kicked out at them, but it was just no good. One of them buried its face in his throat and bit out a chunk of bloody meat in a red spray.

He screamed.

He made a gurgling sound.

Then he dropped the light. It was waterproof and floated in the rippling water, casting a weird glow over its surface that reflected up the walls. He swung and fought, but they kept clawing him until he was laid raw in a dozen locations. Then they climbed him like starving rats, biting and tearing as if they wanted to dig into him. He tried to fire off one last round, but he couldn't make it happen.

In the flickering flashlight beam, he saw why—his fingers were gone, chewed to nubs.

Then he saw the creatures. They were small, primeval things, naked, their flesh pallid and strangely mottled. They were albinos from living in the close darkness, spawning in it like cave rats. Their eyes were bulbous and white, mouths oval like those of sea lamprey, gums pink and set with crooked yellow teeth. Matted white hair hung from their scalps in twisting greasy braids like looping roundworms.

They made piping sounds as they fell on him, more coming out of the walls of the tunnel like burrowing worms.

Kopecki screamed as his blood turned the thrashing water pink around him.

He stared into their cruel, subhuman faces as they made to strike. This was the last thing he saw before they took his eyes, ripping them out by the cords of his optic nerves.

9

Above, it was no better. Confusion became chaos, and it was every man for himself.

Troopers and deputies slammed into each other and handguns were discharged and voices were shouting, screaming. Flashlight beams were dancing around, aimed at the sky, the ground, the mist. Kenney tried to pull everyone together, but somebody slammed into him and pitched him into the ooze and he clawed his way back up, terrified of being pulled below like Kopecki.

Something fast and blurry-white took a State Patrol trooper and yanked him right off his feet into the mist. Kenney could not even honestly say what it was, other than some subjective impression in his mind of a tall white ape and a shock of equally white hair that hid its face.

"WATCH IT!" he heard Hyder cry out. "WATCH IT! THEY'RE EVERYWHERE!"

Kenney spun around with his 9mm and saw more anemic hands coming up out of the muck as the things from below pulled themselves up like corpse worms.

A deputy stumbled into him, screaming in his face.

He saw why: his scalp had nearly been peeled free, his face a red, streaming mask like a child's runny finger painting.

Hyder was right: they *were* everywhere.

Kenney saw a circle of white, grotesque faces; leaping, vaulting forms. A deputy got dragged into the fog by a long-armed shadow. Two more got sucked down into the mud by pale, raggedy things. Semi-human forms came up from the muck like nightcrawlers from their holes and disappeared just as fast.

Weapons were discharged out of pure panic and it was an absolute wonder nobody was hit.

One of the things leaped in Kenney's direction.

He saw red nails streak at his face, and he pumped three rounds into it until it fell back and away.

Another one clawed out of the darkness and a bony white hand—knitted with pulsing, flabby flesh—took Kenney by the arm. He shrieked and struck out at a grimacing, hideous face. He heard the butt of his 9mm Browning sink into a pulpy mess with such ease he thought there could be no bones beneath it. He pulled away and then grabbed the creature by its arm...and it dove into the mud sea.

And was gone.

There was nothing to mark its passing but a sheet of white flesh in his hand, flesh that wriggled and squirmed like it was filled with insect larvae.

He tossed it aside and began to run, fighting his way through the muck.

A deputy nearly bowled him over and he soon saw why. Something was clinging to him, an insane fighting shape like a lynx or a bobcat. It clung to the deputy's neck like a leech, claws firmly entrenched in his throat. Kenney reached out to yank it free, expecting to feel his hand grasp a pelt of dirty fur, but what it got instead was rutted, swollen flesh that came apart under his fingers like wet newspaper. When he yanked his hand away, ribbons of it were tangled in his fingers.

He heard a snarling amongst the confusion.

He turned and there was…a *thing* standing there, only it was no thing, but a child or something very much like one. It was small and rawboned. Long white hair was plastered to its face with mud and drainage. It reached out for him with hooked fingers, a horrible little hobgoblin that had come in the night to tear his bleeding heart out by the roots.

He squeezed the trigger more out of shock than anything else.

The round punched right through it and it made a weird, trilling sound and fell back into the mist

Drenched, sprayed with mud, bleeding and sore and quite beyond any terror they had known before, the survivors bunched together in a defensive circle, back to back and made ready for what might come next.

And the night went on forever.

10

The State Patrol trooper Kenney saw yanked off into the mist was named Carla Sherman. She was not a local, having been born and bred in White Plains, New York, and she had no idea what the hell was going on…other than the fact that it was sheer madness.

She never saw what grabbed her.

She only felt hands that were impossibly strong. To Sherman's credit, she didn't go easily. She used every trick she knew to break free. And when that didn't work, she pulled her Glock 17 and fired three rounds into the leg of her captor. She was thrown to the ground and abandoned. Whoever or *what*ever held her was simply gone.

But the mist held. It was almost phosphorescent, charged with moonlight that lit up the dank, dripping world around her in subtle, wavering, and eerie light.

She could hear a commotion in the distance.

She ran off in its direction and splashed right into a leaf-covered pond that swallowed her right up to the hips. She fought her way free and found herself staring at countless pairs of eyes watching her from the brush. She began edging away, skirting the pond and reaching for her radio. But by that point, she did not know why. There was no way in hell back-up would get to her. They had their own problems.

There was a rustling motion behind her.

She pivoted, bringing her weapon to bear. She saw nothing. Movement off to the right. She was being played and she knew it. Whatever these things were—and she had long dismissed the idea that they were people as such—they were trying to heighten her fear and uncertainty. They were trying to work her into hysteria so she would get confused and make mistakes. And they were doing a great job of it. Beads of sweat rolled down her face. Her hands were shaking. A blossom of cold fear opened in her belly, spreading its petals.

"I'M ARMED!" she shouted. "I WILL SHOOT TO KILL!"

Her voice echoed off into the mist and still she heard sounds from every side, furtive rustlings and stealthy footsteps, a sound of phlegmy breathing. She sensed clandestine motion everywhere but could not pin it down. She was beyond ordinary terror by that point and she was using every bit of her training, experience and resolve to keep down the full-blown panic that was rising inside her like a column of hot air.

She heard whispering.

It was all around her.

At first she could not be sure what was being said, but then it became clear to her. She was being mocked. Mocked by voices that were liquid and gurgling, barely human. *"I'm armed,"* they said. *"I will shoot to kill."* As more and more of those whispering, clotted voices joined in it was almost too much. A scream trembled in her throat, her uniform shirt clung to her back with sweat. A cold chill went up her spine, and every muscle tensed. The whispering continued, low and evil and hissing. There were other sounds…a guttural grunting like that of a boar, then something that might have been a hollow chuckling, and then the unmistakable sound of chattering teeth.

Something broke loose inside her and she began randomly firing into the mist. She put rounds out in front of her, to either side, and behind her with little control or thought until in her panic she realized she had emptied the Glock.

Then she screamed, a long and shrill sound of absolute despair.

And something hit her between the shoulder blades.

It was enough to put her face first into the wet leaves and stagnant puddles. She tried to move and there was a knot of pain at her back. It felt like she might have dislocated her shoulder. *Goddamnit, move! You have to move! If you don't get out of her right now, then...then...*

She forced herself to her knees, banging her foot off what must have hit her: a rock. A big rock nearly the size of a basketball. She climbed to her feet, trying to grab her radio with trembling fingers and she heard a whooshing sound. Another stone. This time it collided with her face. She yelped and went back down to her knees. Her cheek was gashed open. A warm gout of blood splashed down her face.

She turned and saw someone not three feet away.

A woman...at least something *like* a woman. Her eyes were bulbous and blank white, dirty gray hair plastered to her head with water and leaves. Her face was a horror, like a deflated skin bag of ruts and pouches, a viscid sheet of protoplasm that was trying to crawl off the skull beneath.

Carla tried to crawl away, fully aware of the fact that she was whimpering now, dirty and defeated, tears running down her face, her breath catching in her throat. She did not feel so much like a big badass cop. No, now she was a little girl, hysterical with terror. She pulled her legs up and wrapped her arms around them, rocking back and forth as she pissed herself.

The woman hopped closer to her on hands and knees, pendulous breasts swaying back and forth. She had a stick, and kept poking Carla with it. In the belly, the arms, the thighs. She was particularly interested in what was between her legs.

Carla tried to scream, but all that came out was an airless wheezing.

The others were moving in now.

She could see their silvery, moonstruck eyes getting closer as they came out of the fog. And crawling through the grass and wet leaves were…children. Small, primordial looking things that inched towards her like centipedes. They made high, piping sounds like spring peepers, dragging themselves forward on their bellies. Like the woman, they were naked, their flesh unbearably white and streaked with dirt, smeared with mud, leaves in their hair. One of them was dragging what looked like a scarf behind it, but it was no scarf but an undulant, parasitic worm attached to its throat.

The woman swatted her again and again with the stick until it broke, leaving red stripes over Carla's face and arms. Then the woman had her, forcing her down, straddling her. She brought her face in so close that Carla could see the mites jumping in her greasy hair. Her breath was hot and stank like an open grave. Drool fell from her lips, a ribbon of it breaking against Carla's cheek.

Carla lost it.

She tossed her rider and almost scampered away, but hands seized her. What seemed dozens of hands. Her hair was grasped, head yanked back, and the woman came in close again, muttering incomprehensible things in a clogged voice.

Carla screamed for real this time.

But not for long. The woman jammed her white, mucid hand into her mouth, silencing her. Carla gagged, then vomited, but she was held fast. The woman's nails raked against her tongue and then the fingers went deeper and deeper.

No, no, no! Carla heard a voice in her head say.

The woman forced her hand down Carla's throat, inch by terrible inch. Her jaws had to open wider and wider to admit it. The hand probed deeper as Carla shook with a gag reflex, choking and trying to cough it out, but it was no good. An ordinary human hand would never have been capable of such a thing, but the woman and her hand were hardly normal by any means. Her flesh was like rolling wax, the tissues beneath nearly liquid. The hand narrowed and elongated like a snake working its way down a gopher hole and Carla was thankful when she began to lose consciousness.

By then, the woman had her elbow in Carla's mouth and the others could barely contain their excitement.

Her last sensory experience was the distant feeling of that hand down in her belly, rooting around and clawing at things until it clutched something and tore it free, dragging its fleshy mass back up her throat to present to the others.

11

Later that night, an old woman left her farmhouse, sniffed the damp air and considered the dark sky. She knew, absolutely knew in her bones that trouble was coming, trouble like she hadn't seen in ages.

She stood on the back stoop of her house, nervous about going out after dark, as she had been her whole life. Something which had only gotten worse and more deeply entrenched as the years had flown by, like the yellowing leaves of an ancient book. Night was a bad time out on Bellac Road. A time when things that should not be, were, and those that should have crawled like graveworms walked tall like men.

Earlier, she had heard the commotion and the shooting in the night, far distant in the outer reaches of the Ezren land where it butted up to the Pigeon River State Forest. She knew it was the police nosing about and making a fine mess of things, sticking their noses in where they weren't wanted and getting themselves in a fix at the same time. It was only a matter of time. When she had seen that big, dirty bulldozer cutting a path through Ezren lands and peeling up what lie below, she knew it was coming.

They're going to get everything stirred up, that's what they're going to do. We're going to have bad days and terrible nights like we haven't had since—

Eh? Was that a sound? Sure it was. They were out there. She was only glad that the sky was overcast and there was no moon to brighten up the yard and the pasture beyond. The moonlight had a funny way of lighting up their eyes and she did not want to see them. She was three months shy of ninety-six and she could have happily spent what time was left and gone to her grave without ever seeing those eyes again. She had seen them first when she was a child shining like silver coins in the tall grasses, and ever since, they had come in her dreams, bright and forever watching.

She stepped down off the stoop, dragging a hefty bag of scraps behind her, the kind of things they liked. She would put it out for them as her mother had and her mother's mother and on down the line. If they were kept fed, less chance they would start causing trouble.

The old woman paused, three feet from the stoop, just off the flagstone path in the grass. God, it was not so easy at her age. There had been a time when she dragged the leavings out for them and was back inside within a matter of minutes, doors locked and bolted, windows shut tight so she wouldn't have to hear those perfectly awful sounds they made.

Now it took time.

She felt a slight spike of dread in her chest, but there was no real fear because she knew they would not harm her. They were dogs that would not bite the hand that feeds.

As she paused there, listening to the crickets and the peepers calling out, the calls of herons and nighthawks, she thought, *You're too old for this and you know it, but like your mother, you're too damn stubborn to admit it.* Yes. Maybe. Possibly. But she had decided long ago that she was born here on this farm and she would die here just as her husband had some seventeen years previously after a life of hard, honest work.

Not that her children were accepting of that decision.

She had three of them. Only her daughter was left now. Her eldest son had passed of an embolism not three years before and his brother had died in the war. That left only her youngest, and she was always at the old woman about going off to a retirement home.

"You would want such a thing for me?" the old woman would say to her. "Your own mother? You want me to sit around with those old farts, watching them drooling and pissing themselves, talking about days long gone while food runs down their chins and they shat themselves?" She always said "shat," thinking that "shit" sounded undignified somehow. "Is that the life you want for me? Sitting around gossiping with the old hens until I just give up and don't get out of bed anymore?"

Betty would tell her that's not what she wanted at all and explain the benefits of such a place—medical care, activities, companionship. There was a world of possibilities. But the old woman would have none of that because she had watched her own mother die in one of those places.

"And when I die," the old woman told Betty, "it will be of my own choosing, not because I'm locked in one of those prisons."

"But Mom…"

"Don't but me, young lady."

Which was kind of funny, because Betty was sixty-seven on her last birthday, but it did not matter to her mother because she was always going to be an unsure, coltish girl whose head was not screwed on quite right, and didn't have the common sense of a yard mouse. Not that she didn't love her because she did, but her choices were not always the best ones for herself or for others.

"You want me to go into a home? All right, I'll do it on one condition and I think you know what that is, young lady."

At this point, Betty would always shake her head and silently mouth "no" because she didn't want to know, she just didn't want to know.

But the old woman wouldn't let her off that easy. "You move back here, back to your home. You get out of that city and tend to things."

"I don't want to know about any of that."

"It's necessary that food and scraps and meat that has turned be left out for them."

"No, I don't want to know about any of that. I'm not about to leave my life so I can pick up the pieces of yours," she'd say and instantly regret it. "What I mean is...I don't want to know about that stuff. I can't live here knowing that...those things are out there. I just can't. Why do you think so many of us leave and never come back? I don't want to know about Haymarket and its rotten past. I don't."

"That's the problem with you young people—no sense of tradition, no responsibility to the old ways that are the right ways. If those from below are not seen to, they'll rise up and—"

"No, Mother, no more."

Yes, that was how those conversations always began and ended.

As the old woman made her way through the grass out to the edge of the forest, pausing every few minutes because she was feeling her years, she knew that Betty was right in one thing: Haymarket's past *was* rotten. The whole goddamn town was built on yellowed skeletons tucked in closets and mortared with secrets. That's the way it had always been. A great big diseased sore that was now being picked at by the police. They were digging out at the Ezren place and everyone knew you didn't dig out there. It was bad enough that now and again some bones would be found out in the mud flats of the Pigeon during the August dry spell, washed there by the spring flooding. But you didn't go digging for them and not on Ezren lands. Now that sore would open up and its foul blood would start running again.

When she made it to within thirty feet of the trees, she squatted down uneasily and dumped the bag out. The stink of it was appalling, but it was what they liked.

"It's here!" she shouted in a dry rasping when she'd finally gotten back on her feet which took some doing. "Come get what's yours…"

She could hear them out there, rustling about in the underbrush. Worse, she could smell them. And that made her move back to the house a bit quicker despite the protesting of her hips, knees, and bad back. By the time she reached the stoop, she was dizzy from the exertion. Well, maybe she'd sleep through the night for once.

And maybe I'll sleep beyond that right into eternity.

She turned, expecting to see their hunched, dragging forms, but they were shy. They did not like to be seen any more than she liked seeing them. "Come, then!" she cried out to them. "Take what I've offered and go on back with you, back to your slimy holes!"

As she made it up to the stoop and through the screen door, the smell increased and she heard them crawling out of the woods, hissing and gibbering. One of them was giggling.

12

"All I'm saying is that I wish you had practiced some common sense," Sheriff Godfrey said the next morning, his face hard as quarried marble. "Didn't Hyder tell you how dangerous that might be?"

Kenney, his bloodshot eyes staring into dead space, said, "That man's a damn superstitious fool and we both know it."

Godfrey just nodded. "Maybe he is at that. But fool or no fool, none of this would have happened had you just listened to him. Now I got three missing deputies and one state trooper. How in the fuck am I supposed to explain that?"

Kenney just shook his head. He had no answers. After last night, he was clean out. He saw the world in an entirely new way now, divine revelation had been shone upon him in all its grisly splendor, and he did not like it. Not one goddamned bit. You lived through something like that, how did you look yourself in the face again? How did you have any faith in reality? How could you live your life knowing there was madness lurking in every shadow?

Kenney lit a cigarette and looked around the trailer.

The muddy footprints on the floor. The rain slickers hanging on their hooks. A gentle rain was falling as it had been falling all morning and on the roof it sounded like popcorn popping. He could hear men outside, dogs. It was just before dawn when Hyder and he and the others had wandered back to the road. They found their cruisers and got the hell back to the farmhouse, though what they wanted and wanted badly was to drive and keep driving until they were far from Bellac Road and its malignant fields and creeping woods and ruined farmhouses.

Godfrey was sitting at the table, drumming his long callused fingers and staring into a cup of tepid coffee. He was a tall, lanky man, wizened and scarecrow-thin like vellum wrapped over an architecture of coat hangers. His eyes were gray and stern like polished steel, his face a maze of intersecting ruts.

He looked over at Kenney, gave him a withering look. "I'm so goddamned pissed-off at your fucking lack of judgment, Lou, I could shit in your mouth and make you chew it. You know that? The media's lined-up on the road out there. Only a matter of time before our missing personnel problem reaches their ears and then I'll have questions put to me I don't have answers for. Give it a week and we'll have the FBI sniffing around up here and then what we'll have is the biggest clusterfuck since your mama spread her legs and pissed you out." He pulled off his coffee, made a face and set the cup down. "I been sheriff of this county going on twenty-five years, Lou. Twenty-five-goddamned years. And I'll be the first to admit I don't have the answers to everything. But I'm smart enough to know that there are some things I wasn't *meant* to know. Mysteries that were intended to remain mysteries."

"That's bullshit."

"Bullshit, is it?" Godfrey shook his head. "I'm telling you right now, Lou, I'm on my last nerve with you. Maybe you're hot shit down in Madison, but out here you're naïve and goddamn green. What I should do is tell the press and your fucking superiors how you lost four fucking men in a farmer's field. They'd get a real chuckle out of that. By the time they were done laughing, you wouldn't have a damn thing to smile about."

Kenney pulled off his cigarette. "So do it. Maybe it's goddamn time. You people up here have been brooding over something for a long time, haven't you? Maybe it's time to blow the lid off it."

"And put your career into the shitter along with mine?" Godfrey forced himself to pull off his coffee. "Hell, it's probably already too late for that. But I do owe something to the people of this county that elected me and I plan on protecting them if that's even possible now. They deserve better than to have this neck of the woods turned into a late-night horror show."

Kenney had to give him that one. "I suppose."

"You suppose. You've stirred up a real hornet's nest now."

Kenney stared at him through a haze of smoke. "Have I?"

But the sheriff just shook his head. "Oh yes. People from these parts...those that know about Bellac Road and the Ezren place...they know enough to stay away. Most have never seen or heard anything out here, but they're smart enough to trust their instincts. Every summer, of course, we get hikers lost out here and hunters in the fall. But what can I do about that? The Ezren place is posted private property, but you know these assholes from the city, they don't listen, don't respect things. They wander off into the boonies and know about as much about 'em as I do about menstruating. And, so, the missing persons ratio in this county is way, way above the national average. But sometimes, I guess, folks just vanish." He sighed and stared at the wet grayness pressed up against the windows. "When I heard Wisconsin Electric had an easement across the Ezren property, I winced. And when their dozer plowed up some remains, I wasn't surprised. I wanted to ignore it, Lou, pretend it hadn't happened, but I couldn't. I had a job to do, so I got hold of the state and they sent you people up here. You've got a hell of a team there. They're good. So...maybe, maybe this is all *my* fault. Maybe I should've bronzed my balls years ago and took care of this. Maybe."

"Why didn't you?"

"Maybe because I knew better. Maybe I'm smart enough to let things lie. And mostly because my first term would have been my last because people around don't like outsiders digging into their past and parading their dirty laundry out for all to see."

Kenney had mixed feelings about Godfrey.

On the surface, he seemed like a good cop, smart and savvy. But to let something like this—whatever in the hell *this* was— go on year after year was contemptible. Yet, for all that, he almost felt sorry for him. He had been living with this every day for years. Watching more and more people turn up missing and not knowing what to do about it, so he just looked the other way. It was easy to do, he supposed, but sooner or later your skeletons clawed out of their moldy closets and your demons slipped out of their boxes.

Godfrey seemed to think he was protecting his flock by keeping their secret and respecting their ways, but in fact he was sitting on the top of one smelly heap of shit and had been for years. Only now, the stink could no longer be contained.

"What you've got out there is a big graveyard, Kenney," he said. "And we're not just talking the bodies of people that disappeared, we're talking things almost worse."

"Like?"

"Like grave robbery."

"*Grave robbery?*"

"You heard me. Don't act so damn surprised because I know you aren't surprised in the least. We've had trouble with that through the years. And if you wanna go down to the local paper, you'll see it's *always* been a problem in these parts. And you can only blame so much on wild dog packs and the like. Got so the cemetery caretakers don't even report these things. They just bury up the hole and forget it happened."

No, Kenney wasn't surprised, not after Spivak told him some of the bodies appeared to have been embalmed. "That village out there...those ruins. What do you know about it?"

"All I know for sure is that it's like some epicenter for the trouble here. It has a history, a bad history. It's the thing that has blighted this part of the county, reason people won't live out on Bellac Road. Just too many...disturbances."

"But—"

The door opened and Hyder came in. He looked at the sheriff, then he looked at Kenney for a time. He smiled thinly. "How you feeling, Lou?"

"I'll live."

"Sure you will," he said.

For one moment, Kenney was certain that Hyder was going to say, *sure, you will, but not them others whose lives you fucking threw away*. But he said no such thing. He seemed apologetic and sympathetic if anything. His eyes looked on Kenney with acceptance now, understanding, a knowledge that there would be no more fencing between them...certain things had been brought to light and they had both looked them in the face. Comrades. Brothers-in-arms.

But I'm not his goddamn brother. I don't understand any of this shit and there's no way in hell I would have sat on my hands and did nothing while this problem got worse and worse.

Despite his bluster, though, he wasn't so sure of that. What if these were his people? What if he was born and bred in

Haymarket and these people were his own, his roots tangled with theirs? Their history his own? Then what? He just didn't know.

Hyder cleared his throat and said, "One of the search parties just got back, Sheriff."

"And?"

"Nothing. Same as the one I took out earlier today, didn't find shit."

Hyder told them they had tried doing some digging out near the area where he thought the *trouble* had happened the night before. But it was pointless—every time they got down a foot or two, all that rain just washed the muck back in. Even a backhoe couldn't cut through that mess, he said. They got near the village and the dogs went crazy, yelping and snapping, chasing their own tales. Even the handlers couldn't get them near to that godawful place.

"Let's take a walk," Godfrey said.

13

They pulled on their slickers and knee-high Sorel boots and walked out in the chill, damp grayness. Rain pissed down from the sky in whipping sheets. The farmyard was a flowing, sucking mire of mud. The drainage ditches at the sides of the dirt drive were threatening to overflow. Saturation point had been reached—fourteen inches of rain in the past week right on top of ten the week before. Rivers and lakes were overflowing and Northwestern Wisconsin was turning into a flood plain like New Guinea during monsoon season.

The crime scene techs labored on in the downpour. Sixteen sets of remains had now been discovered and there was probably no true end in sight. Spivak, the coroner, was out there, lighting from one tarped set of remains to the next like a flower-hopping bee.

Kenney watched them as rain blew in his face and the trees groaned in the wind, tarps flapping like flags and rusty rain gutters creaking on the upper story of the farmhouse. He'd been at countless other crime scenes, but this one was far worse. It was down inside him, gestating, making him feel worse by the hour. He hated the wetness and the muck and the wind and the mist and that horrid, mephitic odor of violated graves that clung to everything and everyone.

"Come on," Godfrey said, leading them to the leaning hulk of the farmhouse itself.

It was huge and sagging, weathered gray as old bones. It leaned precariously to one side and the porch overhang had been shored-up with 4 x 4s, but still it hung forward like the brim of a tipped hat. Shutters had been nailed over the upper story windows as if they were trying to hold something in or keep something out. The siding had popped free, planks nodding in the wind. Bitter seasons of snow and wind had peeled the shingles free, and they were spilled over the wild grasses like the scales of prehistoric fish. There were gaping chasms in the roof, the walls. The kitchen at the rear had entirely caved-in.

Kenney thought it looked like a house of cards ready to fall. It hadn't been occupied in over thirty years, but it must've been a real dump even then.

"Watch your step," Godfrey told them. "Porch is gone all soft."

Kenney saw fingers of moss climbing between the warped planks underfoot.

They went in. The atmosphere of the place was odious and oppressive. There was a smell of age and rotting plaster, a desiccated stink of ancient animal droppings. It was pungent and gagging. Cobwebs were strung in the corners like netting and birds' nests were visible through great rents in the slouched ceiling. Autumn leaves—brown and curled like the tiny mummified corpses of mice—were blown across the floors. The house creaked and groaned and swayed around them as if it were ready to fall into itself. But beyond that, it was still in there like the belly of a sarcophagus.

Hyder looked from the black mouth of the stairwell to a stained archway that led into a deserted parlor. He licked his lips. They were gray and tight, his face grayer yet, constricted and compressed, corded muscles jumping beneath the skin. "Damn place," he said. "Gets under your skin, don't it?"

Godfrey led them down into the cellar.

It was just as black down there as the inside of a body bag. Kenney forced himself down the steps, flashlight trembling in his fist. He saw the hunched shapes of crates and old nail kegs, antiquated furniture and mildewed cardboard boxes—

He started, thinking he saw something—some hunched-over figure—hobble away from the light.

Hyder was breathing hard. "Sheriff, the men...the search parties...they're concerned about being out after dark. I told 'em you'd call it quits at sundown."

"Sounds good to me," Godfrey said.

There was a brick cylinder blotched with water stains that rose up from the floor. It stood about four feet high, about twice that in circumference. It looked like an old cistern if anything. A flanged lid of rough-hewn planks was nailed in place.

"You wanna know about this place, the things that go on here, Lou, but I can't help you. Later, maybe, we'll go see an old woman who lives up the road a piece—" he said, staring into Kenney's grim face "—but for now, I'm gonna tell you a story. It's a story that I don't want the others to hear."

Hyder looked like he was going to have a stroke.

"You might wanna call this one a horror story," Godfrey said, grinning with a mouthful of yellowed teeth, his face ghoulish and shadowy in the reflected gleam of the flashlights. "We're going back about twenty years now. I'd been on the job a good bit then, long enough to know the sort of shit that pops up out here pretty well. On the far side of Ezren's property, maybe three, four miles from that deserted town out there,

there was a little place called French Village. I say *was* on account it ain't there no more. You can find it, all right, but you won't find no people there. Anyway, it was out on a county fork, stuck straight in the middle of nowhere. It barely passed as a village, more of a hamlet than anything, I guess. Old fellow that lived there—Buckner, I think—called and said he heard some screams coming from a little farmhouse across the way. I was in the area, me and a deputy, so we stopped and had a look. We didn't find shit. Place was empty. I mean completely empty.

"It was eerie, I'll tell you. The evening meal was put up on the table, but no one around to eat it. These were farm people and there was quite a spread—corn and chicken and taters and beans and you name it. Lot of it still warm. A few dinner rolls had been bitten into and some chairs had been pushed away from the table as if the family had gotten up together to take a look at something.

"And that was it. A family of six had slipped into thin air and all they'd left in passing were a few screams. Even the family dog—a big shepherd—was missing. He'd been chained outside and Buckner said that sumbitch was just as vicious as you please. We found the chain—it had been snapped."

"Jesus Christ," Kenney said, lighting a cigarette. "No signs of forced entry? Blood? Anything?"

Godfrey let out a long, low sigh. "Nothing like that. We found some muddy footprints in the living room. The front door was hanging wide open in the wind. There was a muddy handprint on it. But these prints…well, they weren't from what you'd call *human* feet or hands." Godfrey looked pained. "I had Buckner go through the whole thing a dozen times. I asked him why he hadn't gone over there, farm folk being clannish and all. You know what he told me? He said he didn't go out after dark, not with how things were. Said he locked his doors and windows and slept with a twelve gauge on his lap."

"What did you do?"

"Nothing I could do. Not really. A week later, another house in French Village was emptied and nary a clue as to why. Just them muddy prints again. During the course of the next month, two more families vanished in the dead of night. No screams, no nothing this time. Other than that muddy spoor, the only thing that remained constant was that in every case there were clear indications of recent occupancy—beds that had been slept in, coffee poured and never drank, cigarettes burned down in ashtrays. In one case, a shower had been left running as if someone had stepped out to grab a bar of soap. Then, quick as it had all started, it stopped. People were plenty scared by then. Those that were left moved out. Only Buckner stayed…all alone out there in that ghost town. And one night, well, he went missing, too."

"What happened?" Hyder asked.

"Not a damn thing. The investigation continued for years in one form or another, but finally we closed it. We didn't have a thing to go on. But that wasn't the end. About two months after the town emptied, a public works electrician over in Haymarket was down in the sewers where the mains were run and he found something. It was the partial skeleton of a dog, a length of chain still hooked to its collar. It had tags, and they placed it as being the missing shepherd of that first family. The state crime lab boys went over the remains and came to the conclusion that the dog had been eaten and had died sometime during the process. There were teeth marks in the bones and the marrow was missing. They never identified what sort of animal had done it. Not to this day. Of course, what I'm telling you never made it into any newspaper. Sometime later, a couple boys were hiking along a Wisconsin Central spur in the Pigeon River Forest about two miles from here and they found a bone.

They thought it was part of a bear or deer. The police ended up with it. Crime lab said it was a human femur."

Hyder swallowed uneasily. "Was it—"

"Eaten? I don't know. I don't think I honestly want to know."

Kenney stood there in the musty gloom, dragging slowly off his cigarette. "So what are we dealing with here, Sheriff? Let's get our hands out of our shorts and get to it—what the fuck is out there?"

But Godfrey just shrugged. "Who really knows? All I'm saying is that this place has a history, Kenney, a bad history, and things happen out here and sometimes reason doesn't exactly hold up or throw any light on it. This is one of those dark corners of the world you hear about, a place where things are distorted, askew. This place has been like a cancer for far too long and maybe we've been afraid to cut into it for fear it would spread. Well, that's done now. We don't have a choice. But you're the guy with the knife and, brother, you can have it. Because once you start slitting this ugly mess open, I don't envy you what you might find. Some logs, Lou, they just weren't meant to be rolled over."

14

Kenney, of course, had more questions and wasn't too polite to voice them, but he got nothing from either Godfrey or Hyder. They hopped in the sheriff's cruiser and took a ride maybe a mile down the road past a few abandoned farms and their requisite decaying buildings until they found a small farmhouse with a wisp of smoke coming from the chimney.

They stood on a dilapidated porch that groaned and creaked, pounded on a door that shook and trembled. Tarpaper flapped in the wind. A crow cawed mournfully in the sky. The door finally opened just a crack and then exploded wide as if it had been kicked.

"What in the name of Christ do you want here?" an old woman's shrill, grating voice demanded of them. She couldn't have weighed much more than a hundred pounds dripping wet and probably not even that much. Even though she was frail as a bag of twigs, she was grizzled and hard, her face a toothless maze of wrinkles. Two yellowed, bony claws held a twelve-gauge Ithaca pump nearly as big as she was. "You're on private property, you sonsabitches, so get on your way and get now!"

Godfrey said, "Miss Elena...it's me, the Sheriff."

She scowled, adjusting the spectacles on the plug of her nose. The shotgun lowered maybe an inch. "So it is, so it is. And that there…yes, it's Daniel Hyder, Carolyn's boy. And not one stick brighter either." She looked to Kenney. "And you…hmm…nope, you ain't from around here. You don't have the look of a local. I can smell the city on you, son."

They followed her into a cramped, but tidy living room. An ancient Jungers double-burner oil stove percolated in the corner. The air was warm and greasy. The furniture in there had been old forty years before. To call any of it "antiques" would have been gracious.

"How you doing, Miss Elena?" Godfrey asked, because with old people you always *had* to ask that even though you very often regretted doing so.

She offered him a very stark laugh. "How am I doing? Shall I catalogue for you the ways this old body has shat on my doorstep in recent years?" She laughed again. *"How am I doing, he asks. What a thing to ask an old bat like me."*

He swallowed. "Well…how *are* you doing?"

"I'm doing for shat, you idiot. But every day above ground is a good day, my father always said. And I'd rather be looking at the dandelions from above than the tree roots from below."

"That's funny," Hyder said.

"Well, sit the hell down," she commanded. "You fancy a drink? Something hard and hairy?"

Kenney was going to say, no, not on duty, but the sheriff's look told him it wasn't wise to decline what hospitality the old woman could provide.

"This is Lou Kenney," he told the old lady. "He's the chief investigator with a crime scene unit from—"

"I don't give a fancy shat if he's your goddamned lover, Mathew Godfrey," she said, leaning the shotgun in the corner by a stack of yellowed papers and surveying the lot of them with an evil, impatient look like the devil deciding on whose soul to harvest first.

"Lou, this here is Elena Blasden."

"Pleased to meet you," he said.

She scowled at him. "Like hell you are."

There was a smell of wood smoke in the air, a sharp and bitter odor ghosting just beneath it. Kenney watched Elena Blasden cross the room and pull aside a set of dark curtains he assumed led into a bedroom. But it was no bedroom. Just an alcove with stacked, fresh-cut kindling and…a still. It sat atop a homemade rock firebox, a capped iron boiler with coiled metal tubing leading into a wooden barrel. There was a drain tube at the bottom of the barrel, a quart milk jug under it filling with a steady drip. The old lady took out four jelly jars and put about two fingers in each.

"Have a taste, gentlemen," she said. She took a good pull off her own and color swam into her pale cheeks. "Good stuff. A little weak, I'm supposing, but it'll put iron in your pants."

Kenney raised his glass, studied it. The smell was enough to peel paint from metal. He took a swallow and his stomach badly wanted to throw it right back out, but he held it down deep while it burned there in a knot of acid, sending out hot fingers in all directions. And the longer he held it, the better he felt. It was like a broom inside him, cleaning up, sweeping away anxiety and uncertainty and fear. It did a body good.

Hyder gagged, and the sheriff winced like something with teeth had hold of his privates.

"We're here," he managed, "to, to—"

"I know why you're here, Sheriff. I might be old, but I ain't blind and I surely ain't deaf nor stupid. Soon as I saw that tractor plowing a line through Ezren's fields, I knew there would be trouble same as you did. *Progress.*" She turned and spat into a bucket by the stove. "That's progress for you."

While Hyder smiled dumbly and perhaps numbly, Godfrey said, "I want you to tell Mr. Kenney all about it, Miss Elena. He needs to know what we know."

"*We?* Since when do you know anything?"

Godfrey shook his head and smiled thinly. "It's time," he said. "This had to happen sooner or later."

"I suppose it did," she said. "I suppose it did at that." She fixed Kenney with a hard stare, and then she looked back at Godfrey. "Now you want me to unburden my soul to a stranger. You want me to open the trapdoor of Haymarket and let him look upon all those dark, dirty things we hide from the light of day...is that it?"

"Yes."

She considered it. "Well, maybe it is time. God knows, it's been going on far too long." She sipped her 'shine, set it aside, and folded her hands primly on her lap. "Well then, Mister Kenney. Listen good. I'll tell you some things you won't wanna hear nor believe, but I'll tell you."

She ran skeletal fingers through her thinning white hair that looked like bits of blown cotton stuck to a pale pink balloon. "First off, you need to understand that the land over there—a good piece of it out here on Bellac—was owned by a godless clan called Ezren. That farmhouse out there, it was built on the foundation of something much older. A well of sorts, I guess you'd call it. According to local Ojibwa tradition, a huge flaming stone...a piece of star...fell from the sky many centuries ago and burned itself down into the earth. It glowed for sixty days and sixty nights. In fact, they say, at night it not only glowed but shot a green beam of light straight up into the heavens like a beacon to where it had come from."

"A meteor?" Kenney asked.

"It would seem so."

"Meteor*ite*," Hyder corrected them. "When they hit the Earth, that's what they're called. I had a telescope when I was a kid and—"

"And nobody's interested," Miss Elena said. "The Ojibwa shaman considered it a holy object, and they piled stones around the hole it made. They worshipped at it long after its glow had winked out. Story has it, many of them died. And it was here that this holy object becomes an evil object. It becomes taboo, and all the tribe give it a wide berth. Going so far, I understand, as to move the tribe itself several miles away…"

Kenney listened as she went on and on about half-remembered Indian superstitions and tribal traditions. He supposed there could have been a germ of truth in all of it. Perhaps a meteorite *had* fallen and perhaps it was radioactive. That wouldn't have been so surprising. That would explain the deaths in the tribe and the need for them to move far away from it. He had never heard of a meteorite being dangerously radioactive, but he figured it was possible.

"Now how much of that Ojibwa story is folktale and how much is truth is anyone's guess. That brings us to the Ezrens. The last Ezren—Luke Ezren—died off thirty years ago. God save the Queen, what a blessed event that was. He lived in the farmhouse with his mother and his daughter. He was of direct lineage to the ones that built that dead town yonder in the toolies. *The blasphemous place*, as my mother called it. Old timers used to call it Hell's Half-Acre and with good reason. It was built by settlers from out east long before the Revolutionary War with the Brits. See, they came out here, following a British contingent that built a fort out in these parts. Fort's long gone. It fell to the Yanks after the war and slowly went to seed. But the town, it survived, if you wanna call it that. There was a puritan preacher name of Clavitt who founded that place. They called it Clavitt Fields. Him and the Ezrens and the Cooks and

Blake's—they were the original occupants. But it was a fellah name of Corben—Irish or Welsh or some such thing—that came to that town just before the war and started tapping into the darkness that seeped from that well. Before him, well, it wasn't a good place even then, but afterwards? It got that much worse."

"We were out there," Kenney admitted. "Last night."

Her eyes narrowed. "Were you? Then it's still there, by God. And at night? Well, you're either a brave man or a damn stupid one." She took another drink, cleared her throat. "Now, as the years passed that town got worse and worse and there were stories of devil worship and what not. But that was probably horseshit. Those people back then, when they didn't understand something they started going on about spirits and witches and goblins. You know the type. I believe a Hyder was among them," she said, glaring at the Undersheriff. "Anyway, by then other towns had sprung up around here, after the war. Well, things happened—awful things—and on around 1820, 1830, people had had their fill. A group of them from Trowden—Haymarket now—destroyed Clavitt Fields. They shot down who or whatever lived there, knocked down the houses and buildings with cannons from the fort, burned the rest. Seeded the ground with salt. Thought they were done."

Kenney had to remember to blink now. "But they weren't?"

"Hardly. Those that spawned in that evil place, they still lived out there. Maybe in the ruins or below like rats. See, they had become…degenerate, physically degenerate. They were a tainted lot. Weren't exactly human no more before the town was razed, but afterwards…dear God, horrible. That's what, horrible."

"How do you know all this?"

"These are tales handed down through my bloodline. My great grandfather was one of the men who raided that town. I have his papers." She finished her 'shine and sat there, eyes gone filmy with dark memory. "Now, like I said, the town was in ruins, but...*things* still lived out there. Wasn't long before graves was being opened and rifled through, bones found scattered about. Children turned up missing. Men and women, too. Bad business all around. The local Ojibwa wouldn't go anywhere near that place. They bury their dead same as us, but with what was happening, they started burning 'em. Burning 'em so that whatever haunted those ruins wouldn't dig 'em up and gnaw on 'em. Anyway, as you might suspect, a lot of the towns around here folded up. Farms were built and abandoned and it's carried on to the present day. Farms still don't do well around Bellac Road. County people have tested the soil, say it's just fine. But don't believe 'em none. It's just plain bad, particularly over towards the Ezren spread. At night, surely, at night it sometimes has a funny shine to it. Course, livestock disappears and people, too." She looked at Kenney with a penetrating, unflinching look. "Sheriff tell you about French Village? Yeah? Okay, then, you know."

But Kenney just shook his head. "No, I still don't know a damn thing."

That made Elena Blasden laugh. "Nobody really does, son. Around the turn of the twentieth century, maybe shortly before, another Ezren from out east showed up and claimed the family holdings. Bought up a lot of acreage. His name was Charles Ezren, Luke's father. Common consensus was that he was insane, dangerously insane. Figured he had to be to live out there with them that haunt the shadows. And Luke? Yes, I knew him as well as any around here. He was crazy, too. He was in league with them from below."

"What about the mother and daughter?"

Elena sighed. "Daughter was named Rose. She fled after Luke's death, it was said. But as to his mother...well, I don't know. Gossip had it she passed long before he did. One thing was for certain. No one ever saw her, but they said she was not something of this world."

Hyder shook his head. "C'mon now, Miss Elena, I—"

"Shut your damn hole, Daniel Hyder! You don't know your dick from a willow twig!" she snarled at him, shaking one thin knobby finger at him. The tip of which looked sharp enough to spear an eyeball. "Fantasies? Dreams? Is that what? Ramblings of a senile old woman? *Horseshit*. If you've been out there and at night, you know I speak the truth. For it's no horseshit that a group of copper miners not six miles from here disappeared down in a lower shaft. And when they went down to look for 'em, they found the walls honeycombed with holes. Same way this whole countryside is honeycombed. And it ain't horseshit that when I was a girl something came wandering out of those ruins, something that was struck down by a car not two miles from here. Something more grub than human being. Something that was burned, lest anyone dare dig it up to take a look."

Hyder didn't say anything more. Nor did the Sheriff or Kenney.

"Maybe, maybe if the sheriff here feels particularly talkative," she said to Kenney, "he might tell you about Genevieve Crossen's child."

Godfrey just swallowed and looked at his feet.

"If you've been out there, boys, then you know," she said to them, darkness behind her words. "And if you've been out there, can you deny that something lives there *still?*"

But no one could.

She grew angry then calm, agitated then serene. She began to ramble on about "obscene heredity" and "diseased blood," "genetic blasphemies" and "nameless things that walk like men but should creep like vermin". She went on at some depth, her mind drifting in and out of the fog of senility. But at her advanced age, God knew she had the right to lose it a little.

"Think I'm crazy?" she said to Kenney. "Think I'm just plain mad, do you?"

Kenney was going to say that he didn't think that at all, but she just laughed. And that laughter was not a good sort, but bitter and tormented as if she carried the pain of her lineage upon her.

"No matter, Mr. Hotshit Detective. No matter. I say what I say and you can laugh… but I bet you weren't laughing last night, now were you?"

The way she looked at him made Kenney squirm. It was almost like those gray, rheumy eyes could see right into his soul. See all the dark truths and terrible things he couldn't even admit to himself.

"What," he began finally, "what caused this business? What degenerated those people? That meteorite? Some kind of radioactivity?"

Elena Blasden stared at him. But she was looking through him and beyond, at something far distant. "No one can rightly say, son. Only that it's ancient, and it's been here for Lord knows how long. The Ojibwa might have a story or two, but they've never shared it with whites. Only thing I ever heard was something in my family papers, a reference to some old Ojibwa who said that what was down there was from some place where things aren't as they are here." She shrugged. "But that was given just a brief mention and no more. Them injuns is sensible folk. They knew enough to leave whatever it was alone."

Kenney wanted to laugh all this off. Jesus, he'd come here to handle a crime scene investigation and now he was getting tangled up in shit that was just beyond him. Beyond any man's experience. But there was no humor in him. He'd seen things out there last night and, much as wanted to, he just couldn't dismiss all this as local folklore.

Elena Blasden said that—according to the papers of her ancestor, a fellow named Elijah Willen—what was in the well had never been properly named nor classified. Whether it was flesh or spirit, no one could say or no one wanted to say. Just that it was bad, a cancer, a blight, a malignance that had sucked the blood out of the soil over there and from the people of Clavitt Fields.

She said there was only one story in Willen's papers about it. Something concerning a drunk named George Gooden who claimed to have seen something coming out of the well one night. Something he described as being made of "eyes and squirming parts". Elena said that this George Gooden stumbled over to Trowden just about out of his mind, ranting and raving, telling anyone that would listen what he had seen. How it had seemed to glow and flicker, how it had burned his eyes just to look upon it.

"Maybe that George Gooden was just a crazy drunk back then," Elena said. "But there was no getting around one thing."

"What's that?" Kenney asked.

"That what he had looked upon robbed him of his sight, burned his eyes near out of his head. That he spent the rest of his days stone blind."

Maybe it was radioactive, Kenney got to thinking. But right away, he chastised himself for it. Christ, he was a cop. He couldn't let himself be swayed by stories handed down for two-hundred years. What was he thinking? Sure, he'd seen something out in those fields last night, but that didn't mean he had to start swallowing every old wives' tale dumped in his lap.

Be sensible, for chrissake, he told himself.

But being sensible was easier said than done.

"No," Elena Blasden said, "we'll never know about that which was down that well. It may be long gone now, but its legacy is still out there. I know that much."

She told them that according to her great grandfather's papers, it was thought by locals that what was in the well was dormant before Corben came, that he was the one who "stirred it up." Got that thing or whatever it was all riled.

Hyder and Sheriff Godfrey both looked bloodless by this point. Kenney had been watching them, looking for some sign that most of this was sheer nonsense. But he got no such impression. If anything, Hyder and Godfrey looked disturbed, scared maybe. Like little boys afraid of the dark.

Kenney sat there thinking about what he'd seen in those fields and told himself, kept telling himself that no, no, it wasn't possible. Maybe two-hundred years ago when Wisconsin was huddled with black, encroaching forests and Indians and settlers…but surely not now? Not in this day and age.

Elena grinned like a skull. "Let me make it plain for you, son. What you're after…what's responsible for them bodies you're finding…it's not above, but below."

15

After they said their good-byes to Elena Blasden, getting a sour look in return, they dropped Hyder at the Ezren farm so he could attend to his search parties. Kenney and Godfrey drove over to Haymarket and the Sheriff's Department where there was something the sheriff wanted Kenney to see.

In Godfrey's office, once the door was shut and coffee was poured, Kenney sat there and waited for it. Because he knew it was coming and that it wouldn't be good. Whatever in the Christ it was, it would not be good.

Godfrey dug through the bottom drawer of a locked file cabinet and came out with a large manila envelope. He held it in both hands, keeping his eyes on it…like maybe he was afraid of what might come crawling out. "I've had this post a long time, Lou," he said, not exactly happy about the idea. "I've been sheriff here a good many years, and I was a deputy sheriff before that. Somehow, I get re-elected each term and I accept the job and mainly because I'm too damn old to know anything else but law work. Sometimes, though, I hope I'll get voted out of office."

"But you don't?"

Godfrey shook his head. "No, I don't. And sometimes I wonder if it's because I'm doing such a fantastic job...which I doubt...or if it's because I carry a big broom, keep this goddamn county clean. Sweep up all the dirt and keep it hidden away from the taxpayers and tourists."

Kenney just looked at him. "What the hell do you mean?"

"I mean, in this county, being a good cop isn't quite enough, Lou. This job, this post, it asks a lot more of a man than that. It asks him to be the keeper of all the dirty secrets the county cannot or will not admit even to itself. All the filthy, unpleasant things nobody wants to talk about." He dropped the manila envelope in front of Kenney. "And it's always been that way, God help us. Always. So I carry that broom and I do the sweeping, keep the county sparkling, make damn sure nothing awful crawls out in the sunlight where folks might see it and ask questions."

Kenney looked down at the big manila envelope. "And this?"

"What you have there is a file kept by my predecessor, a man named Albert Susskind. Susskind was just another garbage collector like yours truly, as was the man before him and the man before him and so on." Godfrey went to the window, looked out at the gray, moist afternoon, the raindrops rolling down the pane. "That file there has been handed down, sheriff to sheriff, since before the First World War. I heard tell there was another file before it...but it's long gone and that's just fine with me."

Kenney sucked in a breath, let it out. Carefully then, he opened the envelope, dumped out its contents on the sheriff's desk. For the next five minutes, he perused them while a knot of something twisted in his belly. Yeah, here it was, just as Godfrey had alluded to, all the county's dirty laundry. All the things people maybe suspected or gossiped about, but could not prove...and maybe they preferred things that way.

Kenney was beginning to think he might have preferred that, too.

For campfire stories and old wives' tales were easy enough to dismiss, easy enough to tuck in a box and throw up on some dusty closet shelf in your mind. But what Kenney was looking at, this was something else again. What he had was a devil's stew of newspaper clippings, police reports, missing persons files, crime scene notations, and coroner's reports. Assorted photocopied magazine articles and even a few pages from books to round things out. The most recent were twenty-odd years old, and the oldest dated back to before Prohibition.

The newspaper clippings were mostly from the Haymarket *Weekly Mirror*, the Sawyer County *Record*, and the Ashland *Daily Press*.

He began to read...

16

INTO THIN AIR?

August 21, 1958:

Haymarket—Apparently, Charles Nielsen and his wife Clarice have disappeared from their Charing Street home without a trace. Their handsome little brick ranch stands empty some two miles outside of Haymarket. The house is filled with a lifetime of belongings and, according to police, a quantity of cash that "someone deciding to make a run would surely take with them". The only thing peculiar, according to Bayfield County Sheriff's deputies, is that the front door was found standing open and an odd note was left on the kitchen table complaining that "those voices from below" were becoming unbearable...

MYSTERIOUS TRAGEDY

November 12, 1962.

Bayfield County—Donald Brazelton was found dead in his Bellac Road farmhouse Wednesday evening by a neighbor, Douglas Rogers, who claimed Brazelton had been acting oddly for some time. Police report that the Brazelton farmhouse had been completely boarded-up—windows and doors—from the inside as if Brazelton had been afraid of something getting in. Neighbor Rogers said, "I knew something like this was going to happen. I just knew it. I think if I live to be a hundred, I'll never get the sight of Don's face out of my mind—all twisted-up like he was scared to death…"

FARMER'S FIELD COLLAPSES
May 28, 1966:

Bayfield County—Watch your step, so says John Crywck, and he ought to know: on May 26 several hundred feet of his east pasture simply collapsed. Luckily, there were no animals grazing in said area. "It happened in the middle of the night, I guess," Crywck said. "I slept through the whole thing." Upon waking, Crywck discovered that a good portion of his eastern pasture, what he deems is "enough to drop more than one good-sized barn into", had simply fallen into a great central pit some fifteen feet deep. The pit is even now filling with subterranean water.

Old timers in the Haymarket area might recall such a similar episode which occurred back before World War I at the old Bayfield County Cemetery. In that instance, no less than thirty graves and part of the north wall collapsed into a thirty-foot trench due to sub-surface subsidence.

Both of these peculiar episodes bring to mind certain colonial folk tales about the entire region being honeycombed with passages and caves. Dr. Carl Lancer of the University of Wisconsin's Geology Department says there might be a grain of truth to the old tales. "Bayfield County sits on the copper-bearing Keweenaw range of ancient Proterozoic rock. People have been mining copper in both Northwestern Wisconsin and Upper Michigan for centuries," he explained. "There's no doubt that miles of naturally-occurring limestone caves exist beneath the surface, and probably miles of shafts cut out by prehistoric

Indian miners and the later white colonists. Most towns in Bayfield County are probably sitting atop ancient mines. So it's not surprising that the earth might give from time to time..."

THINGS THAT GO BUMP IN THE NIGHT?
June 7, 1969:
Bayfield County—Apparently so. Roger Horsley and family have decided that enough is enough. In 1968 they purchased an abandoned farm on Old School Road bordering the Namekagon River. A prime chunk of real estate with no less than fifty wooded acres. The Horsleys, who had retired from Madison, built their dreamhouse, a beautiful Cape Cod of well over $100,000. Despite continued complaints lodged with the Sheriff's Office, strange things continued to happen on the old farm: The sound of fists rapping on windows and doors in the dead of night, figures seen skulking about the property, voices heard whispering after dark. "Enough is enough," Horseley said. "People will think we're crazy, but they haven't seen the things we've seen. A high-crime inner-city Milwaukee neighborhood would be peaceful compared to this place..."

HUNTERS VANISH WITHOUT A TRACE
November 25, 1972:
Sawyer County—There are oddities and then there are oddities. Not six weeks after two trout fishermen disappeared north of Spider Lake, three hunters, it seems, have joined them. Paul Marsalis, Frank Pence, and Wilbur Stanchely, all of Red Cliff, have gone missing. The three have hunted together for years, according to Pence's wife. She reported them overdue to both Sawyer County and Bayfield County Sheriff's Offices. A search party located their tent camper on the Namekagon River in the northern Sawyer County/southern Bayfield County area. Sheriff's deputies admitted that the camper was "in a terrible

state," the canvas torn and camping equipment scattered about. A great deal of blood was found in the camper and officials are not ruling out foul play. "It looked like the mother of all bears went at that camper," another hunter who prefers to remain anonymous said upon reaching the site with sheriff's deputies. "Everything was smashed and broken, sleeping bags shredded. There were rifles laying around and it smelled like they'd been fired…"

THE STRANGE SAGA OF GHOST-BOY
June 20, 1973:

Pigeon Lake—When it comes to offbeat and spooky tales, Wisconsin has no shortage. Particularly in Bayfield County where the tradition of dark legendry and old wives' tales are particularly rich and apparently still quite active. Well, with that in mind, it's time to add a new chapter: Ghost-Boy. Yes, you heard me right. Ghost-Boy. If you are conjuring up images of Caspar, the Friendly Ghost, then you are way out in left field. For according to the dozen or so reliable witnesses, Ghost-Boy is anything but friendly. Yes, our local haunt has a nasty tendency to knock on doors in the dead of night and peek through windows. He is described by witnesses as being "hunched-over like sort of an evil dwarf or goblin" and having a face "all white and distorted with big yellow teeth". And if that isn't enough to make you sleep with the lights on, consider this: Ghost-Boy's eyes are said to luminous.

A local farmer claims Ghost-Boy has been making away with his livestock…a dozen chickens and Guinea hens and three suckling pigs to boot. That he has found the remains of the animals scattered in the woods. A ravenous ghost, indeed.

But if you're inclined to laugh this off, consider Mabel Willard of Old Pond Road, just outside Haymarket. Mrs. Willard, a staunch and independent widow of 83, says, "I'm not like the others...I ain't afraid to admit there's funny business in this county and always has been. Problem around these parts is that folks are afraid they'll be laughed at. Not me. Laugh all you want, but it don't change things. Folks around here have seen plenty they won't even admit to themselves." And Mrs. Willard, apparently, knows of what she speaks, for Ghost-Boy has made more than one appearance on her property. "First time, I was getting ready for bed when I hear a sort of scratching at the door," she claims, "and then a scraping at the living room window. That's when I saw that awful, grotesque face. Just white and grinning with a big mouth of teeth. I saw it, all right."

So if you're inclined to dismiss this as sheer fantasy, just remember, you've been warned. If Ghost-Boy comes scratching at your window, you have no one to blame but yourself...

MAUSOLEUM VANDALIZED
October 15, 1977:

Pigeon Lake—In what local officials are calling "simply a horrendous travesty", a family mausoleum at the Angel of Hope Catholic Cemetery outside Pigeon Lake has been broken into by person or persons unknown. The perpetrators gained entrance by smashing the lock on the outside of the vault door. Whereupon, they rummaged through the contents of the Goodchild family mausoleum, pulling caskets from their berths and smashing them to kindling. Cemetery caretakers found the atrocity early this morning and immediately contacted the county sheriff. "I hope I never see something like this again," John Pastula, caretaker, said. "Coffins smashed and skeletons tossed to the four winds. There were bones everywhere, dozens and dozens of bones." The sheriff's department revealed that no one had been interred in the Goodchild vault in over thirty years and the last remaining member of the Goodchild family lives in another state. "I've heard about some pretty nasty

Halloween pranks in my time," deputy Sheriff Matthew Godfrey is quoted as saying, "but this is just profane." And profane it surely is. Authorities say they can think of no reason someone would commit such a vile act of desecration...

BOY SCOUTS STILL MISSING
June 10, 1982:
Bayfield County—
For the fourth straight day, Sheriff's Deputies and no less than 100 volunteers beat the brush in the Ghost Lake area just off County Highway M searching for three Boy Scouts from Ashland who disappeared there June 6 on an overnight campout. According to scout master Roger Halen, the troop had set up on Ghost Creek for two days of fishing and hiking and woodcraft. On the night of June 5th, apparently Mike Trombly, 13, and Douglas Kestila, 11, both of Ashland, ventured out after the other scouts were asleep with Troy Bakely, 13. Bakely was found the next morning, wandering up the side of Highway M in something of a daze. He is currently under observation at Hayward Memorial and is expected to make a complete recovery. According to Bakely, he and the other boys had heard stories from older scouts that if you went up to the junction of Ghost Creek and Ghost Lake after midnight, you would "be able to see Indian ghosts coming up out of the ground." Although Bakely is obviously distraught, he claims that both Trombly and Kestila were pulled down into the mud by what he calls "white, scary hands." At this point, Bayfield County Sheriff Albert Susskind said he will not "overlook anything, even the wildest speculation..."

A YULETIDE MYSTERY
December 24, 1985:

Haymarket—Just in time for Christmas, yet another tragedy to fill our overflowing cups with. A sparkling new log home outside Haymarket has been found empty. Gone are Richard Shoen, his wife Ruth and three children. The children reportedly told friends of seeing "weird spooky figures looking in their windows at night". Police are investigating...

SHADOWS IN THE NIGHT
January 13, 1989:

Pigeon Lake—Paul Barrington, a retired Ashland councilman, was rushed to Hayward Area Memorial Hospital after suffering a heart attack. His wife said that "funny things" had been going on around their secluded nineteenth-century farmhouse. That her husband had seen some "weird shape" lurking around an outbuilding and had given chase with a shotgun. He was found in the snow, barely conscious, by his wife. Tracks found in the drifted snow nearby were called "curious, to say the least" by investigating sheriff's deputies...

17

It went on and on. Kenney digested what he could, though he badly wanted to spit most of it back up. And not because he didn't believe any of it, but because he *did*. For he could see the thread running through all of this that Godfrey wanted him to see. And seeing it and feeling its pull, understanding it, made him physically ill. Sure, maybe some of that stuff was bullshit and exaggeration, but not much of it, he was thinking. A week ago, he'd have laughed it off, but not now. Not after what he'd experienced in Ezren's field last night.

His sanity might have demanded that he dismiss it all, but he just couldn't.

"It seems to me," he said, "that you people around here have been sitting on a nasty egg for a long time, hoping it wouldn't hatch."

Godfrey said that was true. "Thing is, Lou, we've known for years, many years, that something needs to be done, but I think nobody wanted to be the first to initiate any of it."

"Well, now we don't have much of a choice."

It would have taken hours to go through the file in any detail, so Kenney just kept skimming, reading over things that caught his eye. Things he figured would come in handy later for nightmares and sleepless nights. He found an interesting clipping from a magazine called *Beyond Science*, which was apparently some sort of paranormal journal back in the 1940s. He began to read.

18

...And from the upper Midwest comes this elusive and interesting tidbit. Apparently, in Bayfield County, Wisconsin, a most unusual body washed up last summer in the Namekagon River near the town of Haymarket. The body was badly decomposed and had probably been in the water some time, but appeared to be that of a man or something like a man. Sheriff's deputies and locals that fished the strange cadaver out claimed that it was horribly deformed and sub-human. Its left leg and right arm were missing, and it had been badly worried by fish and local wildlife, but Mr. John Ponce of Haymarket said, "It wasn't exactly what I would call human...its face was just plain awful and the bones sticking through the flesh were like no bones I've seen before." Ponce went on to say that its face was large and irregular, eyes set in deep bony hollows and jaws exaggerated to horrible extremes. Officials said the body was merely distorted from decay and gases, but Ponce does not agree. "Now and again," he said, "some remains'll turn up in these parts and they're just horrible to look upon. Whatever they're from, they're not men as such." The entire episode brings to mind a set of bones discovered in Bayfield County some fifteen years previously...bones that were odd and elongated with a skull that was squat and bestial. Bones that local officials claimed must have been those of some sideshow freak, though others claimed that it was from a member of some unspeakable troglodyte race that inhabits the region…

19

Kenney took that in, finding revelation. He imagined that most people around the country who read it at the time were either nutty enough to believe it or had too much common sense to give it any credence. He was beginning to feel that he was a mixture of both of those extremes because he *had* to believe yet his rational mind told him he had slipped a gear, that such things could not be. Paper-clipped to the photocopy was a little ditty from the *Journal of the Wisconsin Folklore Society*. With a heavy heart and a need born of practicality to dismiss it all, he read it over.

20

What is particularly interesting, is the age of these tales. There seems to be a cycle of myth extending back over two-hundred years in Bayfield and Sawyer Counties. A cycle that continues to this very day. An absolute belief among locals of a race of nocturnal underdwellers that apparently come up out of the earth through mud and sinkholes to raid graveyards and feed on corpses. One is greatly reminded of the Arabic folktales of the *ghul*, which supposedly haunt lonely burial grounds and devour corpses and the unwary…

21

Kenney sighed, shoved all the papers back into the envelope and just shook his head. He lit a cigarette, ignoring the signs forbidding such things, and just stared at Godfrey. "Okay, you've lived here all your life…have you ever actually seen one of these *individuals?* I mean in the flesh?"

"Yes, but only briefly. I don't doubt they exist, though. There's no doubt that they've been here for a good many years." Godfrey sighed. "I don't bother adding to that file anymore and when I told you that cemetery caretakers around these parts tend to hush up grave robbings and the like, I mean it. But I will say that in the past twenty years or so there's been less and less reports of activity from these things. Maybe they're dying out and maybe they've just gotten smarter. I don't know. Don't honestly care to know."

What kind of attitude was that for a cop? Kenney got to wondering, but then he knew, he honestly knew that if he were in the shoes of Godfrey or any of the other county cops through the years, he would have probably taken the same attitude. What else could you really do? If you started nosing into it, you were bound to face the ire of the locals and you wouldn't get any help from other cops that knew because they were in denial. Which meant you'd have to go to the state authorities for help...and what did you do after they stopped laughing at you?

"Elena Blasden was telling some pretty wild tales," he said to the sheriff. "I guess I'm wondering how much of that is true."

Godfrey shrugged. "It's anybody's guess. Most of what she was talking about was before my time. But that bit about one of them getting run down by a car...that's true enough. At least my predecessor, Albert Susskind, seemed to think so. He didn't actually see any of it firsthand, before his time, but he has the autopsy reports in that file if you care to look."

"I don't care to," Kenney said.

So Godfrey told him. "That happened back in the early twenties. Some fellow named Haynes or Hines was on his way up to Ashland on Bellac and something stepped out in front of his car. He hit and killed it...at least one of them."

"One of them?"

"There were two," Godfrey said with a dry voice. "An adult female and a child. The child was killed instantly, the female only injured. Legs broken, I gather. The child was a male and in its death throes, it vomited up what the coroner later discovered to be human remains..."

Haynes or Hines suffered a mild heart attack and was taken to the hospital where he made a complete recovery. The body of the child, after the post, was cremated. The adult female was taken away to the Central State Hospital for the Criminally Insane, placed in a private, secure ward.

"She lived almost a month," Godfrey said. "And then she died during childbirth."

Kenney almost fell out of his chair. "You mean that fucking thing was *pregnant?*"

Godfrey nodded. "According to Comp, the sheriff at the time, it gave birth to something that looked like a larva…something white and slimy that mewled like a cat. It died within a week. Comp never actually saw the child. But the doc up there, all he would say is that some things were meant to walk and others were meant to crawl."

    Kenney sucked on his cigarette, realizing that by coming to Haymarket and Bayfield County, he had just opened up the biggest, ugliest can of worms in State Patrol history. He had a feeling he'd never get the stink of this one off him.

22

Years back, when her sister Mae was still above the ground and not out feeding the worms at the county cemetery, Elena Blasden would get together with her and a few of the other old girls—Mamie LaRoche, Dorothy Palequin—once a month and have themselves what her mother had long ago referred to as a "tea luncheon" and her father had called "a hen party". Elena always figured it was less of the former and more of the latter because before they were done, the private lives of just about everyone were pecked to death and no dirt was left unexposed. Little sandwiches were served, tea and coffee drank, and the local situation was discussed in some detail. When Elena was feeling particularly charitable, she sometimes even invited Renny Fix, but not often because she was of the mind that Renny was a fool as all her people were fools.

Somewhere during the proceedings, the subject of the Ezrens usually raised its somewhat well-worn head and oft-repeated tales were repeated yet again and usually in low voices as if the ladies were afraid of being overheard. Whenever Renny was present, she would repeat the same story her grandmother had told her so many, many years before when there was still a bloom of girlhood in Renny's cheeks. *You stay*

Nightcrawlers

away from Ezren field if you know what's good for you, little miss, Renny would say, recalling her grandmother's words and imitating her intonation the best she could after those many long summers and longer winters since her girlhood. *Those from below come out under the light of the moon like nightcrawlers after a good rain. They're always looking for children to take down below into their lairs and barrow pits. See that you're not one of them or you'll become like them...creeping in the black earth and feeding on dead things. If you see 'em looking in your window some windy night, do not meet their eyes or they'll take you with them and you don't want that, now do you?*

That was the story she would tell as Elena held court and the old women listened, mouths pursed and eyes wide, the children within them scared again as they had been scared so long before. It was a cumulative effort. Once the subject was broached—Elena figured that was the only reason she invited Renny because she was fool enough to broach it every time—it was added to, built upon, framed and finished with a combination of twice-told tales, local gossip, and utter fabrication.

Mamie would practically drool over every deranged and grisly detail, while Dorothy would need to step out for air because her heart would be hammering so painfully and her head reeling with dizziness. That was to be expected, Elena knew, for she was every bit as dramatic at 74 as she had been at fourteen.

Somewhere during the proceedings, once the cycle of rural myth had grown dull with repetition, all eyes would be upon Elena. Mae would insist that she share those things she knew of and Elena would happily oblige. *My grandmother said it still used to happen when she was a girl, usually during long dry summers when the ticks were bad and the moon grew orange as a pumpkin on clear nights. One of them would be born to a normal family and very* often the mother did not survive the birthing. It was a bloody and horrifying affair. My granny said she had caught sight of it one time, just the one time. She had been where she was not supposed to be and looking upon those things she was not supposed to see. Being a farm girl she was not so naïve as city girls were about the birthing process. She had seen plenty of foal, calves, and piglets brought to term and had been present at the birth of two of her sisters. The mystery of life is no mystery to a girl on a working farm. So she peeked in a window where one of them things was being birthed and what she saw set her to running. I asked her what it was she saw, and she told me what came out of that poor woman was more of a grub than a human baby. In those days, such things were handled by the midwife, a woman named either Starnes or Sterns, I can't remember which. When one was born that was more of below than above, it was taken by her at sunset out to the Ezren field and left there. Soon enough, its cries would bring the others up from their holes. Like calls to like and blood calls to blood.

Long after the sheriff and Kenney had left, Elena sat there thinking on things. Though she was elderly, and her time left on this earth was short, her memory was still as sharp as her tongue. Those tea luncheons were now fifteen years gone, and she was the only survivor of them. Mamie LaRoche had died in a nursing home over in Ashland ten years before, and Dorothy Palequin had preceded her three years before that after suffering a stroke while picking raspberries. Mae had passed six years ago now, going peacefully in her sleep.

There was just Elena now, aged and tired, so godawful tired, who spent her days remembering things lost past and faces long gone to ghost. Her body pained her something terrible these days and today her chest felt constricted. Too much excitement maybe and maybe it was simply time to close her eyes.

Either way, she was accepting of it.

23

They held off going back to the Ezren farmhouse as long as they could. Or maybe Godfrey did. It wasn't that Kenney was starting to call the place home sweet home or anything, but he had a job to do. Godfrey, however, was in no damn hurry. In the sheriff's cruiser, they drove past the Ezren place and through the high arched gates of Bayfield County Cemetery.

"There was something else," Kenney said. "Something that Elena Blasden mentioned. Genevieve Crossen's child. Something about Genevieve Crossen's child."

Godfrey nodded. "Yeah, that's quite a tale. But I suppose, since I've already bared the county's soul to you, you might as well hear about that one, too."

Godfrey moved the cruiser down the winding dirt road, past newer sections of the cemetery with their russet and emerald-colored headstones and brass flagholders, then over a low rise where the older areas were. And here, Kenney decided, was where the real cemetery began. It wound off over mounded hills set with oak and hemlock, a crowded city of leaning crosses and tombstones, broken slabs and ivy-covered vaults, a gray and white profusion of marble both water-stained and wreathed in creeping fungi. Family plots atop grassy bluffs were enclosed by rusting iron fences knotted with morning glory and English ivy. Ancient vaults were set into overgrown hillsides like black mouths. Monuments and shafts poked up from thick, congested stands of chokecherry and brambleberry, staghorn sumac and bracken.

"Somebody ought to clean this place out," Kenney said. "It's getting a little wild."

Godfrey pulled the cruiser to a stop before the vaulted doors of a stone chapel with dark, hooded windows that were set with the gratings of bars. "Sure, somebody ought to. Got just the one caretaker here, county can't afford no more than that. He has his hands full, it's a big place."

And it was.

Godfrey said they'd been burying people there since the beginning of the 19th century and longer, really, since just a few years back a group from one of the state historical societies located the old colonial graveyard of Trowden just beyond the back wall of the cemetery. They chopped it free from tangles of hawthorn, ash, and juneberry, exposing the crumbling flat stones to the light of day for the first time in well over a century.

Kenney sat there, staring at raindrops running like tears down lichen-encrusted markers. "Okay," he said finally. "Let's have it."

Godfrey nodded. "If you want to know about Genevieve Crossen, then I suppose I'd have to tell you about a funeral and a murder. The funeral was that of Genevieve's eleven-year-old daughter, Pearl. And the murder? Well, we'll get to that soon enough.

"Now, we're reaching back some here, back to 1956 in particular, the year I turned thirteen and the year little Pearl drowned out in Deep-Cut Quarry, an abandoned quarry that flooded over as quarries will do. The quarry's still there, sure enough, though fenced-off now, and no one swims it anymore.

Even back in my boyhood before the water turned green and filled with slime and swimmer's itch, it was damn deep in spots and you had to know where you could dive and where you couldn't. See, there's pilings of limestone rising up and you weren't careful, you could bash your brains out on them. But the quarry was full of other things, still is. People drove old cars into it, tossed bedsprings and appliances down there. You get your foot caught on some of those things and you'd never break surface again. At least…those were the stories.

"Nobody really knows the particulars of little Pearl's death. She was fooling around out there, around the edge and must have fallen in, couldn't climb back out. No matter. Later that day, Georgy Blasden and his brother, Franny—good kid, killed in Vietnam, April of '68—rode their bikes out to the quarry to catch some frogs and saw her floating out there. Georgy told me she looked like a fancy doll someone had thrown away bobbing out there…I suppose she did at that. See, Genevieve used to dress little Pearl up every day in fancy, frilly outfits, take the strap to her if she got dirty. Poor thing.

"Well, anyway, they fished Pearl out and laid her to rest here, just over aways from where we're sitting right now. It was a very sorrowful thing. After that, none of us kids were allowed to swim in the quarry…even though we did, secretly." Godfrey paused there, the memory of it all filling him, making those lines on his face stand out like crevices in dry earth. "Well, as you can imagine it was all too much for Genevieve. See, that lady had suffered horribly. Her life was nothing but a tragedy from beginning to end. She'd had a son, too, Randy was his name. I barely remember him. He joined the Marines and died over in Korea, October '52. There was, as you can guess, quite an age difference between Genevieve's children…but back in those days with no true birth control beyond keeping your legs closed and your Johnson zipped up, shit just happened. You never knew when. Regardless, in the end, they both died awful, dirty deaths.

"Randy's passing had been tough on that family, so tough that Henry Crossen, Genevieve's husband, started to drink like a fish, trying to wash the taste of his son's death out of his mouth. But he never did. Two years after Randy came home in a flag-draped box, one December evening in '54, Henry piled his '48 Chevy truck into a tree out on Bellac and joined his son. He was hammered, as you can imagine, and after he hit that tree, the truck rolled over, slid down the hillside through the snow and right into Ten Mile Creek. Ten Mile wasn't frozen over completely that year and the truck went through, coming to rest on its roof. With his injuries which were pretty massive, I understand, Henry couldn't get out. And that's how he died…in a cab full of freezing water. When they found him there the next day, he was frozen solid. I heard they had to use saws and axes to cut him free.

"Too much, it was all too much, as you can well understand. Genevieve buried her son, then her husband, and finally her daughter and this within an ugly four-year stretch. She went soft in the head and who could blame her? Who could honesty blame her? People kept clear of her and her place, out on Wedeck Road, which is now just called County Road 707. She was just the crazy woman, and you kept away like maybe what she had was catchy. Well, about three months or so after they buried Pearl, strange things began to happen. Stories began to circulate, and they were damned unusual."

Kenney looked at him, almost afraid to ask. "What sort of stories?"

Godfrey swallowed then swallowed again. "Well, people were saying that they'd seen Pearl…seen her walking around out in the woods."

"Jesus Christ."

"Yeah, bad stuff, it was. But you got to remember the way this county was and still is…cut off. Nothing but a lot of small towns and farms with a lot of dark woods and thickets in-between. People liked to talk, people liked to make up crazy stories. A lot of adults in Haymarket had heard the tales, did what they could to keep it from us kids…but we found out. What we heard was that Pearl's ghost was walking around out there, haunting the back roads.

"Now, I should preface this by saying that my old man was on the county board and my Uncle Tommy was a deputy sheriff—lived next door to us—so there wasn't much that happened around here they didn't know about. Well, one moonlit night, I was laying in my bed and it was warm so I had my window open. Just laying there, not sleeping, listening to my old man and my Uncle Tommy drinking beers and laughing out at the picnic table in the back yard. It was after midnight, I remember that much, when this car comes swinging into our drive, horn blaring. Somebody climbs out, ranting and raving and it took both my old man and my Uncle Tommy to settle him down.

"Who it was, was Alan Kresky, and he was drunk. Drunk and rambling, just scared out of his wits. Through my bedroom window above, I heard it all. Alan said he'd been coming back from Luanne Shields place out on Cricker Road, over towards French Village. He said he saw something, something that scared him white. It took him some time to say exactly what. Well, Alan was an old barfly and had been since he got back from World War II and nobody had to ask what he'd been doing out on Cricker at that hour, because both my old man and my uncle knew—just as the whole damn town knew—he was out there putting it to Luanne and had been for some time. Everyone knew that. Even we kids knew that. Old Luanne played it free and easy and the only one who didn't know that was her husband, Bobby, who was out on the ore boats eight months of the year. Shit, as boys, we would hike out to Luanne's after dark and watch her doing it through the window...sometimes with some guy and sometimes by herself.

"Anyway, Alan was out in the backyard and he was just blind...hell, I could smell the rye on his breath from my second story window. I knew that smell of booze just fine, thank you very much, because the summer before, me and my pal Johnny Proctor got into his dad's homemade chokecherry wine and spent the night vomiting out in a pasture. So, Alan was pissed, but what he'd seen out on Cricker had scared him so bad that he'd drove drunk right to the deputy sheriff's door."

"What did he see?" Kenney asked.

Godfrey sighed, studying the battalions of tombstones around them. "Said he saw Pearl Crossen walking up the side of Cricker Road easy as you please. You would've thought that my uncle and old man would have laughed at him and tossed him in the drunk tank, but they didn't. Maybe it was how he looked—I couldn't see from my window, of course, but his voice was bad, like somebody had pulled out his soul, spit on it and shoved it back in—and maybe it was because they'd heard that story too many times by then and were starting to wonder themselves. And maybe, just maybe, it had something to do with Genevieve herself. How she was crazy and haunted, made people real uneasy by then...like the ghosts of her family were slinking around her like hungry cats. She'd come into Haymarket now and again, just out of her head. See people on the streets, ask them if they'd seen Randy around or how she had to get to the tailors and get Pearl's dress ready for her birthday party, but she had to run on account Henry was coming home and she had to get his supper on.

"At any rate, I heard my old man and uncle telling Alan he was drunk and was probably seeing things. But Alan said he wasn't, he'd seen Pearl, she'd come back just like folks were saying. So Uncle Tommy said, all right, all right, maybe you saw some girl walking out there, but it wasn't Pearl. But Alan said it was her, all right. And how did he know? Simple…the dress. It was the dress, he said, that fancy silk and lace dress, bright blue. Well, that carried some weight because little Pearl, as I said, was always prettied-up by Genevieve like a china doll. Shit, when they pulled her from the quarry it looked like she was ready for Easter dinner or her first confirmation.

"Alan insisted it was Pearl. She had been walking funny, kind of limping or something, and she was carrying some animal by the tail…a dead cat. You can just imagine what it was like for him out there on that moonlit road at the witching hour, seeing a dead girl shambling about with a roadkilled cat. Jesus. Now, I don't honestly believe that my old man or uncle really believed that Pearl Crossen had kicked her way out of her casket, but something weird was going on and it had gotten to the point that they couldn't ignore it anymore.

"See, lots of people were telling that same story and lots of people were getting scared. Too many nasty tales were circulating about Pearl Crossen. People had seen her walking the back roads at night same as Alan Kresky, funny look about her, hunched-over and kind of hopping rather than walking. They'd seen her outside the gates of this very cemetery, crouching in drainage ditches, you name it. Mort Strombly said…I'll never forget this…that he'd come upon her out on Cricker at three in the morning. That she'd been chewing on a dead dog at the side of the road when he saw her and he'd nearly put his truck in the ditch. That when his headlights hit her, she looked up at him, her face all smeared with something black and filthy, and her eyes had been yellow. Shining yellow. And her face…well, Mort said it was all wrong, sort of crooked, jutting forth like the skull beneath was trying to chew its way out. Barney Hoke, this older kid we knew, said he'd been out parking with Leslie Strong and Pearl had come right up to the car. Said she looked like something out of a horror movie...like a living skull with greasy hair tangled full of sticks and burrs and dirt spattered over her face and lots of mangled-up teeth. Barney said that both he and Leslie started screaming, couldn't help themselves. Pearl put her hands against the window—it was raining, so the windows were up, thank God—and Barney said those hands were swollen, white and sticky, looked like toadstools. He said they couldn't see her clearly through the raindrops on the window, but whatever that thing was, it wasn't Pearl."

24

"Well, as you can imagine, we kids were getting pretty randy at the idea of this monster in our midst. We wanted to see it. We just *had* to see it."

"So you went up to the house," Kenney said, knowing that was exactly what he and his friends would have done.

Godfrey looked pale, worn out. "Yes. Yes, we did."

Kenney sat there, letting the sheriff build up the strength to tell him this part, to gather the necessary momentum. He knew he didn't want to hear this anymore than he wanted to hear the rest, but Godfrey was going to tell him and probably because he had no choice.

The sheriff licked his lips, his face tight and colorless. He looked to be on the verge of confessing great and terrible things. "Yeah, we went up there. Me and Johnny Proctor, my partner in crime. We were young and stupid, Lou, but not so stupid that we were going to go up there at night…no, I don't think we had the balls for that. We hiked up there, mid-afternoon, hid out in the bushes and just watched that house. It was a warm September afternoon…Labor Day, I think…but we were shaking, just scared shitless, trying to build up the nerve to sneak up to the house and have ourselves a peek. I'm guessing we would never have gotten the nerve on our own, but fate took care of that for us. We saw Genevieve Crossen come out on the porch. She just stood there. We thought maybe she knew we were there or something. I wanted to run, but Johnny said no, just wait. Christ, you should have seen that woman. She'd always been the sort to have her hair done just so, a nice dress on…well, that had gone south. She was dressed in some old stained and wrinkled frumpy housecoat. It looked like a potato sack. Her hair was sticking up and, even from that distance, I could see her eyes, damn, wide and staring and fathomless like sinkholes dropped in her face. Even from across the yard I could see there was nothing left there, Genevieve Crossen was mad…or had been *driven* mad. She stood there for maybe five minutes, not moving, then she stepped off the porch, went around the house and off down the trail behind that led out to the creek.

"Johnny said that was it, that was our chance. It was a ten minute walk back to the creek, so we had ourselves twenty minutes or more to do what had to be done. And honestly? I didn't want any part of it. The air was hot and sour-smelling around the Crossen place and it made something inside me shrivel. But Johnny didn't give two shits about that, he pushed me out into the side yard and we slid up close to the house. We waited there, breathing hard. Then we went up to the porch. And the crazy thing was, although we'd only come to peek in a window, we were now going to go inside and we had decided that without so much as a word.

"The porch. I remember the boards creaking…I can hear them even now, those planks settling under our weight. There was mud and dirt on the porch itself and all over the door…like someone had been walking around out in the swampy lowlands and had brought it back with them on their hands and feet. The Crossen place wasn't some ramshackle old farmhouse that you see around these parts, it was a clean and trim two-story, real nice. Genevieve was just as particular about its appearance as she had been about her daughter. That dirt all over everything…well, it wasn't right and I knew it wasn't right. Something about it scared me, disturbed me. I know we were both thinking that it wasn't from any swamp or bog. No, it was dirt Pearl had dragged back from the graveyard with her.

"So we both stood there, afraid deep down, shivering on that warm day and wanting so bad to run off, but not daring to. We'd sworn an oath of sorts as boys will do and we couldn't go back on that. Johnny took hold of the doorknob and it was open. He looked at me and pushed the door open and it creaked like it hadn't tasted oil in twenty years. A sharp, grinding sort of creak that went right up our spines. The sound of it made something in me shake itself like a wet dog. Maybe it wasn't as loud as we imagined, but it was certainly loud enough to announce our arrival. If anyone was there, they knew we were coming.

"Inside, there was just silence, a heavy sort of silence that made the breath in your lungs sound very loud. And there was a stink in the house…a hot and black smell, a rotten stink of bones and worms and bad meat. Nothing living could smell like that and if it did…well, it would be bad. Real bad. And all I could think about was what Barney Hoke had told us, what he'd seen looking into his car. The memory of that dried up the spit in my mouth. Because I didn't know if I was really up to it, I didn't know if I could look at something like that and not lose my mind. I kept picturing Pearl coming up from the cellar, horrible and twisted and grinning like one of them zombies in *Tomb of Terror* or one of them other horror books we read back then."

Godfrey paused there, sounding breathless. His mind was taking him back to 1956 and it was like yesterday, all too clear and lucid. He was experiencing it all, feeling it all, throwing open doors in the back of his mind he hadn't dared open in fifty-odd years.

Kenney lit a cigarette, waited. He felt like a swimmer with a concrete cinderblock chained to his ankle…no matter how hard he kicked, he could not break the surface, could not find the light and air and sanity again. Forever he would drift in the murk. That's what coming here had done to him. It had robbed him of something vital he would never again find.

Godfrey said, "We heard a sound, me and Johnny. A creaking floorboard up over our heads, a sort of shifting or dragging sound. We knew that we were not alone then…someone was with us and I had the crazy, unshakable feeling that they *knew* we were there, that they were waiting for us above. Together, Johnny and I went up the stairs to the second floor, side by side, wired together and inseparable. Maybe it was just all the negative energy in that place arcing and snapping, maybe it had magnetized us together. Regardless, we got up there and looked down the hallway, struck—at least I was—by a sense of, I don't know, a sort of a neutrality, if that makes any sense. What we had heard wasn't there. There was no one on the second floor but us. Then Johnny elbowed me and I saw, God, I saw, all right."

"What did you see?" Kenney said, tense himself by that point.

"Dirty tracks, old dirty tracks on the floor and they led down the hallway, led to a set of narrow steps at the end. Those steps led up to the attic, and that's when we realized that Genevieve was keeping her dead daughter up in the attic. The passageway going up there was narrow, we had to go up one at a time. Johnny led. We had no weapons except for my pocketknife and a stick Johnny had picked up in the yard. He was carrying it like a club. Quietly as we could, we went up those steps to a closed door at the top. The steps themselves were just filthy from dirty, bare feet.

"Going up there took everything I had. I was sweating and shaking, trying to swallow down something like a scream knotted-up in my throat. There were dirty handprints all over the door and we started to hear sounds from behind it...like the sliding of bare feet, the subtle creak of a floorboard. Like something in there, something was trying real hard to be quiet. The smell was enough to pull your guts up and out...sickening, gassy, decayed. I'll tell you right now that I was scared shitless and the memory still scares me shitless. Johnny reached out and turned the doorknob and as he did, we heard something come drifting out from the other side...a high, hoarse giggling. A cackling like that of some old storybook crone with a dark, terrible secret she wanted to share. It was bad. I think I might have whimpered, I don't know, but that sort of laughter...it was just horrible, wizened and deranged. Maybe Pearl had been eleven years old when she died, but what had gotten inside her down in the grave, it was old...ancient, insane. Evil, maybe.

"God knows that ragged, hysterical laughter had put ice in my blood. A puppet would laugh like that, Lou, about the time it woke up and realized it was alive. It should have been enough to set us running, but Johnny wouldn't have it. It wasn't enough. He was white and sweaty, eyes wide and wet, but still it wasn't enough. He had to see. So he kicked that door open and a blast of reeking, humid air hit us like something rolling from a slaughterhouse or an open grave. It was black in there, just a bit of light coming in through a boarded-up window near the roof peak. I...I can't be sure now. I was so scared. It felt like I was filled with electricity. I wanted to throw up and scream and laugh and just fall down and cry. Maybe all at the same time.

"As I said, it was awful dark in there and it just stank bad like spoiled pork and wet earth. I heard a dragging, metallic sound, and I realized it was the sound of chains. And then that giggling again…girlish, yet profane, obscene. I knew whatever was up there was even then slinking out of the shadows to meet us. Just as I knew we were going to see something that would turn our hair white, something that had crawled out of a grave, black and stinking and wormy. If it was Pearl…then death and resurrection had yanked her mind out by its dirty roots. That's when it spoke to us. And I can't be really sure if I actually heard it or it was in my mind, but I can remember what it said: *'Cmon, Johnny…c'mon, Matty…I've got something I want you to see, something I want you to touch, to feel…'*

"And then? Well, she stepped out of the shadows, got as close as she could with that chain around her ankle. I'm pretty sure I screamed. She stood there, hunched-over and dwarfish, like a living skeleton in a fancy dress that was just filthy and flyblown. And that face…leering and wicked, like something sunk in a pond, worked by leeches and tunneled by worms, white and puckered with a gray, grinning mouth full of narrow, overlapping teeth that were brown and black like she'd been chewing tobacco and graveyard soil. She held her arms out to us and the flesh hung off her fingers in loops. And when she spoke, her voice was clotted with earth, *'There's a place for you below, a nice place for good little boys…'*

"Well, we ran. We fell down the stairs or maybe we didn't, all I know is that suddenly we were in that hallway below and I was certain she would come drifting down at us in a patch of fog like a vampire in an old movie. But she didn't. We could hear her up there, pulling on her chain, grunting and shrieking and laughing. But that was all we heard. We ran out of there and I don't think we stopped running until we made Haymarket."

Godfrey was real quiet after that, panting and mopping sweat from his brow with a hankie, just staring out the window of his cruiser, off through the headstones maybe to where Pearl Crossen was buried. After a time, he said, "I can't be sure even now how much of that really happened. I was scared, Lou. God, I've never been that scared since. We never told a soul about that, at least I didn't. Johnny's family moved down to Chicago not a year later and I've never seen him since."

Kenney let himself breathe. It was quite a story. "Okay, but that's not all. Something…I mean, something had to be done about that *situation*."

Godfrey nodded. "There's not much else, but I'll tell you. This is what my Uncle Tommy told me two years before he died. My old man refused to ever speak of those days. He took them to his grave with him. About a month later, everyone had had enough. Uncle Tommy, my old man, and two other deputies went out to the Crossen place. Tommy said it smelled out there, just as I remembered. The long grass in the front yard, he said, was full of bones…not human, mind you, but animal—dogs and woodchucks, skunks and weasels and bobcats. It was horrible. All that roadkill Pearl had been dragging home, I guess. Genevieve saw them out there and came out onto the porch with her husband's old .30-30 and put it right on the trespassers in her yard. They told her to lower that goddamn rifle and she said she would do no such thing, but they had better get off her property before she ventilated their asses for 'em. Tommy said Genevieve looked like hell, dirty and stinking, hair all wild and eyes wide and bloodshot. Tommy claimed he saw something peeking through the shuttered attic window.

"What you got up there, Mrs. Crossen?" he says to her. "What you got inside that house?"

"Wouldn't you like to know, Tommy Godfrey," she says back at him. "What I got I ain't sharing with nobody. You get your own."

Now it was my old man's turn: "You got Pearl in there, Genevieve?"

"You never goddamn mind!"

"Dammit, Genevieve," my old man says, "Pearl's dead, you gotta know she's dead."

At that, Genevieve just laughed. "So you say, so you say. But you don't know, you don't know anything. I knew'd it were my baby when she wandered into the yard. And since she come back…it's never been so good."

"Tommy said he knew then, as maybe he'd been suspecting all along, that Genevieve didn't really have Pearl in there. You see, what it was was one of them things from the ruined village, one of them from below. A young one, a female. It wandered into the yard as Genevieve said and Genevieve, just plain out of her head, adopted the thing. Cared for that little horror. Loved it and dressed it up like Pearl. But, dear God, it wasn't Pearl, it wasn't even human."

"What did they do?" Kenney asked.

"Nothing they could do. They left. Maybe they could have gotten a warrant, said Genevieve was crazy or something. She surely was. Regardless, they just got the hell out of there, weren't sure what to do. But then something happened that brought it all to a head."

"What's that?"

"A child disappeared. A kid named Ralph Blodden. I knew him. His old man ran the Exxon station in Haymarket. Ralph disappeared one night and the facts are pretty tangled-up, but I'm guessing he wandered out after dark and went missing. Two days later he still hadn't shown. What I tell you now is from my Uncle Tommy. He got it from Willy Chalmers who used to run an apple orchard outside Haymarket. Willy told my uncle this story when he was dying of cancer, figured he had nothing to lose. Nothing at all. Wanted it off his soul, I guess.

"What happened was, people were pretty much up at arms about the Blodden kid gone missing and it didn't take much of a leap on their part to tie it up with Genevieve and Pearl. So they went out there one night with guns and cans of gas and dogs. I think you know what happened next. They found the Blodden kid in a shed behind the house, just hanging there, seasoning up I guess. Willy said he was getting pretty ripe...whether Pearl killed the kid or Genevieve did, figuring she had to provide for that ghoul she thought was her daughter, nobody knew and nobody gave a shit."

No, Kenney figured, *I bet they didn't. I'll just bet they didn't.*

Not that he blamed them for what he knew was coming next. Something had to be done and the law was pretty much useless, so Willy Chalmers and the boys—probably liquored up to give themselves the sort of steel that would be needed—did the job themselves. A small town and its horrendous secrets. You just never knew, never suspected the sort of things crawling under its surface. And most towns had secrets, Kenney knew, dark, awful truths kept buried so the townsfolk themselves could sleep at night.

Godfrey sighed. "Genevieve came out on the porch and Pearl came with her. Willy didn't describe exactly how the girl looked, only to say that she was full of worms, crawling with bugs and her eyes...that's what had stayed with him all those years...eyes shining yellow and behind them, something terrible. Genevieve told the child to get inside. The men were crazy and she knew it. Guns started going off. Willy said he didn't know who fired first, but Pearl took two or three rounds and Genevieve took a few more. A shotgun blast tore her belly open. Pearl...that thing...dragged her *mother* into the house and the men started dousing the house with gasoline. It was an old place and it went up pretty quick. Willy told Tommy that his last sight of Pearl and Genevieve was when the house was engulfed by flames. Through the blazing doorway, Pearl was holding Genevieve's corpse, screaming and cackling and shouting out awful things and then the roof came down on them and that was it. They burned up with the house."

25

Kenney swallowed. "At the time...was there an investigation?"

"Yes, a speedy one, Tommy told me." Godfrey was grinding his teeth. "I remember when the Crossen place burned. I remember it very well...people were glad. They talked about it real quietly for a day or two, then purged it from their minds. It was like a tumor had been burned out. They were content that the house and what it contained was history."

"One last question," Kenney said slowly. "When you went into that house...how did *Pearl* know your names?"

Godfrey smiled thinly. But not for long. He shook his head. "That's troubled me badly over the years, Lou. I don't have an answer for it. Maybe those from below have gifts of a sort and maybe what's inside them, maybe it's something that don't belong here."

Kenney didn't argue the point. With what he'd heard and what he'd seen...who was he to argue anything? If somebody told him the moon was indeed made of cheese, he'd simply ask if it was Munster or Pepper Jack, and was any good in party dips. Reality had been shattered. He believed and he didn't believe. He knew something had happened here, some genetic degeneration had overtaken the people of Clavitt Fields, that their descendants crawled like worms through holes in the earth. He accepted that, much as he wanted to completely dismiss it.

"Well, Lou," Godfrey said, sounding satisfied, "now you know it all. All the things this town, this county has kept secret. It's high time this shit ends. I've broken the sacred trust given me by every sheriff who held this post before me. And you know what? I don't give a happy shit. I'm glad it's out. That file in my office is going into my woodstove and when all this...*madness* comes to light, I'll be just as ignorant as anyone else."

"It's getting dark," Kenney said, without knowing why.

The shadows were elongating, bleeding out in nighted pools from crypts and monuments and thickets of blighted trees.

"We should go," Godfrey said. "But, being that you're in charge of this investigation...what do you plan on doing now? Or should I even ask?"

Kenney sat there, noticing how the shadows were netting the cemetery, how they seemed to sprout in unwholesome tangles. "Oh, I think you know what comes next, Matt. I think you know very well."

26

It was funny how as age advanced you could know things you couldn't know before and funnier still how you could see the truth of things that you had long been blind to.

Elena could remember when her husband, old George, was dying, how he laid that final week on the couch, refusing both doctors and hospitals, saying in his breathless voice how he would either shake off what plagued him or it would be the end and if it was, it wouldn't be such a bad thing. He accepted nature's way and didn't believe in fighting the inevitable. He was a farmer and the good earth was all and everything to him. He had turned it and seeded it year after year and never was there a happier man than he when his hands were covered with black dirt. Maybe that's how it was. A woman had her children, but a man had the earth that he tilled and sowed and reaped.

As he lay dying—something she refused to accept and something he was perfectly comfortable with—on the couch, covered in the frayed quilt his mother had made them as a wedding present, she refused to face the fact that he would soon be gone. He was old, he was tired, he was used up by the land and by life. Not only were his hands callused by long years in the field, but his entire body. His eyes were no longer young and bright, but unfocused and dimming with that peculiar rheumy shine to them like those of an old dog remembering long golden summers many years gone. Yes, she knew what was coming, but she did not want to know. He had been the only constant in her life for so many years that the idea that he would soon be memory was not something she could let herself consider realistically.

But George had known.

Oh yes, he had surely known just as he knew that no doctors or hospitals could change fate or alter nature's plans for him. They could delay it and turn him into an invalid, who would shit his pants and have to be spoon fed, but the course was set and he wanted to face it with a certain degree of dignity.

George knew just as Elena knew now.

This was the final year, the final month, the final week, and—she was certain—the final day. The pain in her chest was tightening by the hour and her old lungs were having trouble drawing in a breath. It was close now. The shadow of death was edging ever closer, and she was too weak to stave it off.

George had been dead for years now, seventeen to be exact, and his namesake, her oldest boy, Georgy, had been gone for three. She missed them both, but mostly she missed Franny. He was her youngest. A kind boy, sweet, sensitive, and wonderful in nearly every way. He had joined the Marines in 1967 and been sent to Vietnam in April of '68. He never came home. And this was the greatest pain she had ever known and one that had never left her. Though he had been gone forty-five years now, his death was only yesterday to his mother, and she still saw his smile and heard his voice and the pain of it all, dear God, it still cut deep.

A smart boy. She could tell Georgy and his sister, Betty, that all that business about the Ezrens and the ruins were just spook stories twice told, but Franny did not believe it.

"There's monsters over there, isn't there?" he would ask. "Things that live under the ground." To which she would always reply that that was plain foolishness. Monsters. Nothing but stories told by weak minds and there was no more to say about it than that. There were no such things as monsters and he was certainly old enough to know that, now wasn't he?

But Franny could never be put off quite so easily.

Maybe such pat little rationalizations would work on his older brother and sister, but never him. He was far too smart for that. He tended to question things. Which always got his father's ire up because he thought Franny simply thought too much, questioned too much. Such things were unthinkable to George who was a creature of instinct and impulse.

"But, Mom," Franny would say, "if there are no monsters, why do you leave things for them? Why do you put out scraps as offerings every night? Why do you feed them if they don't exist?"

Of course, Elena had no answer for that. Not really. She would just tell him that she put the scraps out for the forest animals because they needed to eat, too, and if worse ever came to worse and times were tough, the family would be eating those animals so she wanted them fat and healthy.

It was thin as hell and Franny knew it. But he would consider it and then later, always later when she thought he had forgotten about it, he would ask, "Why is it easier to tell lies than to admit the truth?"

"I don't know what you mean," she'd say.

To that, Franny would only smile as if she had just confirmed his worst suspicions.

Sitting in her rocking chair by the window, remembering and remembering, Elena missed that boy terribly. It still broke her heart to think of him wasted on some dirty battlefield in another senseless war.

Breathing was getting difficult now. She knew she should call Betty but Betty would nag her to death about going to the hospital and Elena did not want that. The end was close, and she wanted to face it as George had faced it: peacefully with no drugs to blur her perception of the next world.

27

There were eight men down in the cellar of the Ezren farmhouse that afternoon. Hyder and Godfrey, Kenney and Chipney, an assortment of state and county cops who carried pickaxes and crowbars. Electric lights had been strung up now, but the place was still gloomy as a crypt. It had about the same ambience, too. Water was seeping from the foundation stones and the masonry was dropping away in wet clots.

Godfrey said, "I guess we're going to do this, then?"

Kenney didn't look at him. He was looking at the cistern set in the floor. "This can't be the original well that Elena Blasden mentioned. This isn't that old."

"No," Hyder said. "You can see it's been worked on."

"Probably old Charles Ezren. Maybe he fixed it like this," Godfrey said.

The shaft of the well had been reinforced with concrete, a metal flange placed over the top. Gray, splintered boards with spreading water stains had been bolted over it. From the looks of it, that was many, many years ago.

Kenney stood there, a cigarette dangling from his lip, wondering why anyone would build a house atop something like this. But after hearing what Elena Blasden had to say, not to mention everything Godfrey had showed him and told him, he supposed there were *reasons*.

"All right, boys," Godfrey said. "Have at her."

Stripped down to shirtsleeves, the deputies with the pickaxes started swinging and the wood came away in damp chunks, rotten through and through. They kept swinging and chips kept flying and soon enough the others with the crowbars got into the act. Within ten minutes, the first boards came free. And with them, like breaking the seal on a moldering coffin, came the smell. All the men in the dank, shadowy cellar were used to the smell of death; the farmhouse and its fields were ripe with it. It got on your clothes and in your hair. It got so you could taste it every time you swallowed.

But this…a hot and boiling fetid stink, a black and pervasive odor of putrescence.

"Jesus Christ," Kenney said, turning away, his belly rumbling with waves of nausea.

Everyone backed away, complaining as the stench filled the cellar like some toxic sludge. A few of the younger men started gagging. One of them broke into dry heaves that didn't stay dry for long. It was that sort of smell. Even blocking your nose didn't seem to help for it laid over your skin in a slimy sheen.

Hyder looked like he'd just swallowed a dead mouse. He kept his distance, a funny look on his face like he needed to vomit and couldn't find a bucket.

Well that's it, isn't it? Kenney found himself thinking. *That's what dirty little secrets smell like when you finally bring them into the light. Did you boys think the stench would be any less? That all your lies and secrets breeding down here in the damp, darkness would not smell as rotten?*

Godfrey was watching Kenney. "You got something on your mind, son?" he asked.

But Kenney shook his head. No point in saying anything, no point in stirring the pot…what was wafting off it was bad enough as it was. Yet…he couldn't help feeling angry at these people, their backwoods ignorance and clannish bullshit. *We got us a fat, filthy black tumor on the underbelly of this county, boys, so let's just keep quiet about it, feed that sucker in the darkness and see how big it gets, see how far the infection spreads and how many lives it destroys. What say?* Jesus, it was that very sort of thinking that had created all this and was making Kenney do what he was now about to do and, thinking about it, he hated every one of these peckerwood John Laws for being too goddamn afraid to do their duty and cut this cancer out by the roots like they should have fifty years ago…or a hundred and fifty.

"Christ, what a stink," Chipney said. "Smells like roadkill on a steam tray."

A couple of them men laughed, then gagged, laughed, then gagged yet again. Yes, that about summed it up.

Kenney and Godfrey sucked their revulsion down deep to where it was manageable and took up the crowbars. Breathing through clenched teeth, they worked the remaining boards free. The last few came apart in their hands and dropped down into the blackness with splashing sounds. Rancid fingers of putrid reek misted from the mouth of the cistern like smoke from a smoldering crematory pit.

Kenney shined a flashlight down there. The beam barely cut the miasmic blackness. It reflected off water down deep. It looked like a room or passage opened up at the bottom of the shaft.

"Must be a lot of bodies down there," a deputy said, "to smell like that."

Hyder just nodded. "Yeah, or a lot of *something*."

Godfrey had one of the deputies go and fetch about fifty feet of rope and a brick. He tied the brick to the end of the rope and lowered it down there like an old-time depth marker. When he hit bottom, he pulled it back up and measured three feet of wetness on the rope.

"Not too deep," he said, looking at the pinched and dour faces around him. "I guess...I guess somebody has to go down and have a look."

28

Six of them went down.
   Kenney, Godfrey, three deputies that volunteered—Iversen, Beck, St. Aubin—and Chipney. All willing to throw caution to the wind for a taste of something that they'd never forget.

Kenney didn't like Chipney going along because he was due to get married whenever and *if* ever this clusterfuck was wound up. He did everything he could to talk him out of it, but Chipney just said, "Now what kind of cop would I be if I turned tail now, Chief? How the hell would I be able to look at myself in a mirror if I didn't go? Don't leave me out of this one. I want to see same as you want to see. Shit, I *have* to see."

There was no arguing with that, so Kenney didn't bother.

He could have ordered him not to go, but Chipney was his friend. They'd caught more shit together than your average public toilet. Leaving him out would have been an insult, even though a voice in the back of his head kept saying, *he's going to die down there and it'll be your fucking fault. You know that, don't you?*

And he did. God yes, but he did. If Chipney really didn't make it, then he hoped he wouldn't either. The idea of facing the kid's fiancée took his breath away.

They took riot guns, their service revolvers, flashlights and extra batteries, handpack radios and emergency flares—though Godfrey warned them about lighting them with the gases down there. They wore waterproof chest waders and black rubber M17 military-issue gas masks. You never knew what sort of crap you might suck into your lungs in that charnel pit.

They lowered a thirty-foot collapsible ladder down the hole and it hit bottom with little to spare.

Godfrey went down first as the others pulled on their gas masks. When it was Kenney's turn, he went down gradually, wondering vaguely if he'd ever see the light of day again and refusing to think about it. The rungs were slippery with the waders on, and he descended cautiously. They wore rubber gloves that came up to their elbows, but were snug enough in the fingers to make for easy manipulation of equipment. They were designed for handling toxic substances.

Near the bottom, Kenney paused.

He could hear a litany of squeaking and squealing, splashing and clawing. It rose up and then faded. The hairs on the back of his neck stood up.

"Rats," Godfrey said, his voice oddly hollow coming through the voicemitter of his mask. "Gonna be a lot of 'em, I suspect."

Rats, Kenney thought. *A lair of fucking rats. Bone-pickers and carrion-eaters. Some that walk on four legs and some that walk on two.*

Then he stepped into the water and it was thick and oily like some greasy soup of rot and decay. It gave off an oily reflection and was patched with floating mats of fungus. Flashlight beams played around through the haze and everyone could see they were in a room chipped from bedrock. A tunnel wound out from it like a gateway into hell. Kenney stepped forward, flashing his light about. Water was seeping from the roof, the walls. He could hear dripping sounds in the distance, little else.

"Shall we?" he said.

"You first," Godfrey said.

Kenney moved forward and the others fell in behind him, the younger guys muttering amongst themselves. All Kenney could smell was the rubber seal of his silicone nosecup and was glad of it. A clump of earth fell and struck the top of his head and he jumped.

The others laughed.

The atmosphere was straight out of a tomb: stagnant, aged, and unpleasant.

There was a low, stealthy noise ahead. He paused, trying to identify it, but there was nothing. Nothing at all. Only the dripping of water like something heard in the depths of a cave, which was pretty appropriate, he supposed. Still, he was not convinced because he knew there had been something, a sound of stealthy movement. Whatever had made it, apparently knew where they were but it wasn't going to show itself until it was damn good and ready.

"This is pretty bad," Beck said. "Can't say I like it none."

"I find that hard to believe," Iversen said.

There was a bit of nervous laughter, but it didn't last.

Godfrey turned to Beck. "Son, you want to head back? If you do, nobody here's gonna think less of you. And I mean that."

"Sure," Chipney said.

The deputy shook his head, looking like a Martian invader in his gas mask. "No, I'll be all right. I was just mentioning the fact."

They moved forward again. The tunnel angled off to the right now, and they plodded on in absolute blackness. The seepage was up to their knees and seemed to be getting deeper, but gradually.

"Place is cut straight through the bedrock," Godfrey said. "Imagine the time this took. I wonder if Ezren did this...Christ, the work involved, it would have taken a hundred men with drills."

But Kenney shook his head. "No," he said. "I don't think it was Ezren. This has been here since long before him I would guess."

But he didn't dare speculate as to *who* might have channeled it out.

The lights picked out the floating bodies of dead rats, leaves, twigs, and a few pink nameless masses no one had much interest in identifying. To Kenney it meant that there had to be an opening somewhere that led up into the light. Maybe in the ruins. He could see beady, luminous eyes that scattered whenever he put the light in their direction.

"I think we're getting close," he said with a grim, gnawing apprehension.

The water was down around their calves now and things were jutting from it—a few skulls gone gray with sludge and mildew, the remains of a spinal column, the broomstick of a femur.

Nobody was surprised by any of that.

They expected bones, and they expected things much worse than bones.

They pushed on and the floor began to dip and the water began to rise. Their hearts sank lower into some bleak morass with every step. They heard something ahead—a quick, splashing sound—that was certainly caused by no rat. They stood stock-still and listened. It was gone.

Kenney stood there. The riot gun and flashlight in his fists felt greasy, like they wanted to slide from his fingers. He clutched them even tighter...the idea of being down there without a light or a weapon was absolutely frightening.

"We should keep moving," Godfrey said as if it was the last thing he wanted.

The water was up to their thighs now. The tunnel arched away to the left and terminated with a door set into a stone frame. They approached it cautiously. It was incredibly old, fringed with mold, its planking rotting and staved-in.

"Why would somebody put a door here?" Iversen asked.

But nobody had an answer. Kenney ran his gloved fingers along it, wondering how old it was. It was blackened and filthy, the latch long ago rusted and fallen away. You could see the hole where it had been set.

He tried to push through it, but it wouldn't budge. Either it was too warped or something was pressed up against the other side. And he didn't want to know what that might have been.

"Give a hand here," Godfrey said.

A cluster of hands pressed up against it and it started to move. On the count of three they gave it one last heave. The wood was so soft it began to buckle, to disintegrate. Kenney put his hand right through one panel and snatched it back quickly, afraid maybe that something would grab it from the other side. Five or six beetles crawled over the palm of his glove. He flicked them away. They got the door open maybe two feet and squeezed themselves through the aperture.

Their lights discovered the room within. A rectangular structure with walls of mortared sandstone that had gone a dirty brown in color. They were patched with huge, spreading mildew stains that were black as oil. The stones jutted forth in a crazy, uneven patchwork. There was another doorway that led into yet another tunnel. The ceiling was low and dripping, but in the center of it, a passage like a chimney led up into the gloom. They flashed their lights up there, but all they could see was the filthy stonework and the narrowing throat of the passage, what looked like an ancient metal grating high above.

The entire place reminded them of some medieval dungeon and they couldn't guess at its purpose. The water sluiced around their waists, and they moved cautiously for fear they would step into a hole and get sucked into some nightmare abyss.

Godfrey touched the wall, and it came apart under his fingers. The mortar had the consistency of wet cement, the stones they held dropped into the water. "Goddamn place is coming down around us." He moved forward, examining the rough-hewn walls in some detail. "Imagine the time it must've taken to build something like this! Christ, years and years and years!"

"But it's not going to last much longer," St. Aubin said. "We'll be lucky if we get out of here without this whole damn place coming down on our heads."

"If you want to go back, you can," Kenney told him.

"We should *all* go back and I think you know that."

Godfrey pulled another stone out, pressed the barrel of his riot gun through the chasm. It met with no resistance. He crouched down, shining his light through there. "Christ, there's another room in there…oh, holy shit." He stood back up, sighing. "There's skeletons in there…"

Kenney pushed through the knot of deputies, got his light and his face in the chasm. He saw a narrow room with a sloping ceiling. Some it had caved-in. Rubble was heaped everywhere, shelves of stone rising from the murk like the humps of a whale. He saw the skeletons. Ancient things, yellowed and blackened. They were leaning against the far wall and against one another, water slopping around their rib staves. Had to be twenty or thirty that Kenney could see. But nothing recent. Some of them were so old they had literally fallen into themselves. A few skulls were nowhere to be seen.

Beck kept shaking his head. "All those bodies up there and all this down here...skeletons...oh Christ, Sheriff what is this all about?"

But Godfrey just shook his head, his eyes wide and unblinking behind his face shield.

Kenney removed a few more stones. Mortar fell away like clods of wet soil. He could see pretty good in there. He panned his light around, knowing full well if he lived through this nightmare he would see that chamber and its occupants in his dreams for the rest of his life.

He was remembering what he'd seen in the fields that night, what he'd sensed in those spectral ruins, what Elena Blasden had said, and he thought: *They raided Clavitt Fields, destroyed the town and what lived there. But they were wrong, horribly wrong. Because those people were scarcely human then, and all they did was force them underground into this labyrinth. And that was nearly two-hundred years ago. Almost two centuries of living and inter-breeding in the damp, sunless darkness, where they became something far less than human, a species unto themselves. And their progeny have survived to this day, mutating into things more like worms than people, creatures no longer equipped for open spaces and sunlight. Only at night do they come up, and then only to hunt, to dig, to feed.*

Jesus in Heaven, what must they be like? What have they evolved into? Things like Genevieve Crossen's adopted daughter...or worse?

He could picture Charles Ezren and then later his son, Luke, bringing people down into the darkness for them. Bringing them food. He didn't know that to be true, but from what he was seeing it was almost a foregone conclusion. All the remains they had found thus far pointed to the fact that what lived down here in this sunless labyrinth were ghouls, eaters of the dead.

"All right," Godfrey said. "Let's move here."

They fell in behind him and he led them through the tunnel on the other side. But it was no tunnel, but more like a crevice, a gap between two buildings. The walls were fashioned of squalid, crumbling brick, water seeping from them in slow, steady rivers like leaking faucets. They had to turn sideways to squeeze through. The water came above their waists now, moving with turgidity more like gelatin than water. Dead rats washed by, other things they refused to look at.

"What the hell is that stuff?" Chipney said.

They'd all been wondering that because they had seen masses of it floating about—some pinkish, pulpous material that looked like bread dough, save it was vaguely transparent. Only here it was not floating but growing right up the walls in fleshy seams.

"Some kind of fungus," Kenney said.

St. Aubin went up to a vein of the stuff and touched it with his hand. Even through his glove he could feel it was warm. "It's moving," he said.

Kenney and the others put their lights on it.

"That's crazy," Iversen said.

"Fungi don't move," Godfrey pointed out.

But as Kenney got closer and investigated it for himself, he saw that St. Aubin was right: it *was* moving. It shuddered when he poked it with the barrel of his riotgun. It shivered. Despite his aversion to it, he touched it lightly with his fingertips. It was pulsating slightly with a gentle rhythm not unlike that of a newborn.

"We don't have time for nature study," he said, leading them on.

He got no argument. None of them wanted to know anything more about this subterranean world than they absolutely had to. And he couldn't blame them on that count.

They were here to search for missing cops. That was their job. It was the only thing that needed to concern them.

By that point, nobody was saying much of anything and Kenney knew they were scared shitless to a man.

They were hearing other sounds now, and they weren't just cavorting rats or the subterranean network flaking away, but a lunatic, congested whispering. He could remember it from the fields that fated night and down here, yes, down here it was much worse. A tenebrous choir in this spirit-riven pit. It grew louder, faded, rose up again and took on the resonation of a high, evil cackling and then fell away again. Echoing and echoing.

The crevice widened and they stumbled into another chamber. More of the fungi hung from the ceiling like Spanish Moss. Kenney brushed against some of it and he could almost swear it was crawling.

The water was a black, surging pool in which countless shapes bobbed and drifted. In the glare of the lights, everyone saw bloated bodies and parts of them—limbs, trunks, a head or two stripped to bone—coming apart in the filthy, putrid water, leaving oily wakes on the surface as they putrefied.

One of the deputies started retching. Another made a low, moaning sound inside his mask. Yet another just trembled, his entire body shaking. Kenney and Godfrey looked at each other and kept looking. They were communicating something, but neither really wanted to know what that was.

Kenney stared down at the head of a woman that bumped into him. Her skullish jaws were sprung as if in a scream. A full main of greasy hair fell over her skinless face. He could see a gold cap on one of her molars. He began to shiver.

Three tunnels led away into the wall. One of them was caved-in completely.

Kenney looked up at them and they beckoned to him, offering a long, unpleasant death. "Two roads diverged in the yellow wood," he said and his voice was flat and empty and somehow alien even to him.

"What's that?" Godfrey said, maybe a little more harshly than he'd intended.

But Kenney just shook his head. "We either turn back…or we split up and keep going. Your call, Sheriff."

Godfrey gave him a near-psychotic look. It was no easy feat ordering men to their deaths. But he did it and hated himself for it.

29

Godfrey led Beck and Chipney down the passage, splashing forward in the dirty water. The passage gradually widened—like a birth canal, he thought—until they reached another room in which bloated things broke the surface like islands, only they weren't islands.

"Bodies," Beck said, as if that needed saying at all.

They studied them in their lights. It was appalling. Like a rumba line of floaters, all of them bloated and waterlogged, and each one seemingly a bit more decayed than the last. Flies lit from them in black, buzzing clouds. They wriggled with maggots, ribbons and sheets of flesh trailing from them in banners. The insane and disturbing part was that they did not seem to be individual cadavers, but parts of a greater whole.

As Beck and Chipney pulled back, Godfrey kept his stomach down where it belonged and moved slowly towards them, though it was honestly the last thing in the world he wanted to do.

When he got to the nearest one, he prodded it with the barrel of his riotgun. It shuddered in the water, sending out slow torpid ripples. Flies rose and fell, maggots dug in deeper. All that was bad enough, but he noticed that the body—man, woman, who could say?—was connected to the others by rubbery strings of tissue. It not only connected the bodies like fish on the same stringer, but it grew up and over them, a morbid white material that looked soft and spongy.

More of the fungus.

God, it was everywhere down here...floating in little islands and glistening humps, growing up out of the water in threads and webs and knotted creepers. It made Godfrey's skin crawl, and he was damn glad that he had the mask on. The last thing he wanted was for the younger boys to see how absolutely fucking terrified he was. The fungus was unnatural and he knew it. It had proliferated down here and seemed to be everywhere as if they were inside of it, inside of some mammoth fungi that owned the netherworld.

"It's eating the remains," Chipney said.

Godfrey's gas mask shook back and forth. "Yeah, sort of breaking them down."

Chipney shivered.

Godfrey moved away from the bodies towards the nearest wall. He studied it in the light bracketed to the barrel of his riotgun. The brick was dark and stained, moldering with some black slime that seemed to be eating away the mortar. He jabbed a finger of his glove into it and it was soft. Slime dripped from it. But none of that concerned him. He was more interested in the stratum of blubbery pink fungus that grew between the bricks, bulging from cracks and crevices like greasy dough.

I bet if a man were to stretch out and take a nap down here, he thought, *that he'd wake up netted in that shit. It would grow all over him.*

He was no stranger to death.

He knew that the most disgusting things happened to bodies that were underground, away from the air and sunlight.

Things fed on them. Things grew from them. But he'd never seen anything quite like this.

His throat dry as sand, he moved over to a large clot of the stuff that bulged out like a rubbery bubble on an inner tube. The shit looked like it was moving. It could have been his imagination, but he did not think so. It was pulsing slightly. He pulled a lockblade knife from his shirt pocket, unfolded it, and jabbed the blade into the bubble.

It moved.

A ripple passed through it like a clenching muscle.

The blade had slit it easily enough and from the wound a few droplets of some scarlet juice leaked out.

Is it bleeding? Is that shit blood?

"Hell are you doing, Sheriff?" Beck asked.

"Nothing, just nosing around."

Beck was clearly agitated. "Well, no disrespect, sir, but let's just get this done. I'm sick to my stomach and my fucking skin's crawling."

"All right, son."

Hell, who could blame him? Who could blame anyone from getting their backs up in this awful place? Godfrey felt pretty much the same way himself. How could you *not*?

He was terrified and sickened just like they were.

Christ, it felt like his stomach had grown legs and was trying to walk up the back of his throat. But as nauseous as it all made him, as claustrophobic and uneasy, he was still fascinated by it all. Those stories that had made the rounds of Haymarket and the county for so damn many years…this was the epicenter of it. Down here in this stinking, misty blackness. This was the black beating heart of it, the core. How many locals had ever been down here and lived to tell the tale? And how many men or women, for that matter, had ever reached the fountainhead of a legend?

Lots of 'em have through history, you just don't hear about 'em because they never come back to tell the tale.

He moved towards the far end of the room, the others falling back behind him. He stepped carefully, very carefully. As he passed the line of bodies, his wake made them move and drift and he thought he heard Beck whimper in his throat.

Hang tight, son, he thought. *This is going to get worse and you know it.*

There was a passage ahead and he entered it first, his light filling it, making shadows jump and cavort. He let out a little cry and fell backwards, almost tripping and going down in the water.

Beck and Chipney were at his side immediately.

"What is it?" Chipney asked.

Beck was breathing too hard to ask anything.

"A rat…I think it was a rat," Godfrey lied. "A goddamn big one. It jumped out at me."

Beck shined his light down there. "Nothing now."

"No, we must have scared each other. Sorry to startle you, boys."

Godfrey stood up from the sloping wall where he'd been leaning. It had taken every bit of strength he possessed to conceal from them what he had looked upon. When he had first entered the passage, his light had picked out the shape of a man…something like a man. A hunched-over, ratlike form that was grotesque to the extreme. There had been something growing from its belly like sacs, sacs that looked oddly like baby doll heads, but hairless and white and mouthless.

Then it had disappeared as if it never was.

"Maybe we should go back," Beck said. "This is getting too…too fucked-up for just a few men."

He was right, entirely, but Godfrey said, "We got missing cops. I'm not calling this off until I know what the hell happened to them. They'd do the same for me, I hope."

"Definitely," Chipney said. "We move on."

Godfrey got on the radio. Down there with all the stone and brick walls, the reception was shit. He got Kenney, but it was mostly static. Hyder, above, came in a little better, but not much. Godfrey knew just as Beck and Chipney must have suspected that the farther they penetrated into the labyrinth, the worse the reception would be until there was no reception at all.

His heart in his throat, he led them deeper into the passage.

To what waited for them.

30

Now it was the eyes.
       Dear God, what next?

Elena was still in her rocking chair by the window and it didn't seem she would ever leave it now. This was her last sitting. She had been feeling poorly when she sat down, wanting to be in her old favorite rocker by the window feeling the sun streaming onto her old skin, warm and golden. It had never truly occurred to her that she would never get up again, that this was the last time she would lower her frail old bones into her beloved chair.

She had sat in it through so many years since George had made it for her just after World War II. She had rocked babies in it and tended to midnight feedings in it and watched through the window as she did now for George to come back out of the fields as evening set in. Yes, yes, yes, many years, all of them fluttering in her head now like the pages of a book, granting her a peek at their worlds, their memories, but not much more than that and she had to think that it was for the best, strictly for the best.

She had been sitting there for many hours and her tired old body refused to budge an inch. Whenever she tried, her body ached and her muscles failed her, that pain digging deeper in her chest and her breath barely coming.

Oh, the years, she thought, *all the wonderful years and bad years and empty years.*

Her mind drifted in and out and she knew she should have called Betty while she had the chance. It would have been a comfort to speak to her one last time, to hear her voice. But it was not to be. It just was not to be.

She focused her eyes.

She needed her sight because she wanted to see what there was to see right at the end. She wanted to see who carted her away because she knew that one would, one she had not seen in many, many years and one she had never gotten to know.

1916 was the year she was born, and it made her smile when she thought of the gulf of time between then and now and all she had seen. The pages of her book flipped in her mind, one page after the other. *Flip.* It was 1947 and George and the neighboring farmers were raising the big barn out near the crick. It took many days and weeks and still more days to finish it and paint it. George had been prideful of his barn. Then in 1963, it was struck by lightning and burned to the ground along with most of their livestock. That had been a hard year. *Flip.* It was winter, 1939, and Auntie Keena had gone through the ice of the well-named Lake Hardship. They had a funeral for her and stood around an empty plank coffin. Her body would not be discovered until spring. *Flip.* It was 1924. Elena was eight years old, and that summer was the summer when the man with the doll came to town. He was a drifter. He began luring girls off into the woods because he claimed that he had a doll that could smile. Elena and Bissy King had been walking down the road out near Five Mile Creek with jars of fresh picked blueberries and the man had come up to them. His clothes were ragged and his teeth were yellow like rat's teeth. He bowed to them and said, "Ladies, you will not believe what it is my pleasure to possess." He gave them the spiel about a doll that not only smiled but laughed. Bissy went for it, but not Elena. Elena ran and Bissy called after her, "Where you going, 'lena?" And Elena did not know, but she needed to get out of there fast because something about the drifter made her belly feel like it was filled with black ice. The drifter did something to Bissy in the woods and she was never the same after that. She became sullen and quiet, then mean in high school. She died just shy of her 21st birthday in Chicago with a needle hanging out of her arm. *Flip.* It was April of 1968 and there was a knock at the door. George was out in the fields. Elena answered it and a found a Marine standing there. Franny had been killed in action. *Flip.* It was 1922. Elena was five years old going on six and her mother was set to deliver a younger brother or sister. Elena herself was excited, singing and skipping about. She was the only one. The other kids were worried and would not say why. The adults were grim as gravestones. The women from the surrounding farms had gathered as they always gathered when there was a birthing. And late that afternoon, the midwife, Mrs. Stern, had come. Elena never liked her. She dressed in somber gray, her hair pulled back into a severe bun, her lips wrinkled and her eyes like chips of the blackest coal. She did not think it was her imagination that everyone—even the men—were uneasy around her. Towards supper time, her mother began to cry out, screaming bloody murder, and it was within the hour that the child was born. No one was allowed to go upstairs and see it. Only a few of the farm women and the midwife herself. Elena heard it crying out more than once and she asked the other kids if babies always sounded like mewling cats. *Flip.* It was 1996, and they laid George to rest. And although Elena was sad, she did not cry like the others at the funeral. For some reason, she thought the very idea of crying for her husband after he'd lived a long life of good deeds and productive years was near to blasphemy. So she did not cry. She knew he would be proud of her and the pride they felt in one another through years both lean and fat meant a great deal to them. *Flip.* It was 1922 again. That baby was really mewling by eight that night and Elena found her father crying and asked him why, but he would not tell her. And when she asked if she could see the new baby, he just shook his head. "There are reasons you can't see it. Very good reasons." And it was near on to sunset that night, that Mrs. Stern finally left, carrying a small bundle close to her breast. Later, it was said she had taken it out to Ezren Field. Elena and the other children were told that the new baby died of crib death and wasn't that just so sad? It was a boy, and he had been named Edwin. They had a small, dignified funeral out at the County Cemetery and everyone wept as a tiny, empty box was lowered into the ground.

"Gah," Elena said, coming to herself.

Where had she been? Out visiting the years, traveling the long lost roads of her life, all the darkening streets and narrowing county forks and long forgotten footpaths that made up a life and its travels. Oh yes, oh yes. She was not long for this world and she knew it. The idea gave her pain, but it also gave her a certain sense of freedom for the way had not always been easy, and the trail was often stony. If the preachers were right, she would see George again and, oh God *yes*, Franny. He would be waiting there for her as she remembered him before the U.S. Marines had wasted him and made his death into something dirty and ugly.

Her eyesight was dimming.

Her heart was slow and weary in its cadence.

Her lungs fought for each breath.

She was exhausted beyond the limits of her frail old body and soon the darkness would come and sink her into timeless depths. As she realized this, she thought, *I was young once. I was clear of eye and my hair was like harvested wheat. The sun caught it and made it shimmer. The girls envied it and the boys desired it. I had many, many friends, and we danced and sang and laughed, and now I'm at my end just as once I was at my beginning, and my mother held me tight in her arms against the world.*

31

Kenney thought, almost casually: *I'm going to die down here.* And it should have terrified him or sent him scurrying like a rat through the darkness and back to the ladder, but it did not. Some twenty feet into this newest vaulted passage, the water cold and viscous around his waist, he paused and thought about it all. He saw the faces of his two ex-wives, his daughter, his mother and father now long dead. He could remember good times and sunny days and his childhood and how strange it was that it would end down here in this flooded crypt.

And thinking these things, he paled, knowing something important and necessary in him had now given up.

Don't be a fool. You've got plenty of years left if you keep on fighting. If you want to give up, you might as well do it now.

But he wasn't about to do that. Hell, no.

He turned to Iversen and St. Aubin, both of whom followed at a healthy distance as if they were waiting to see if anything happened to him before proceeding.

"It could get bad," he said to them, his bobbing flashlight creating unnatural, sliding shadows over the walls of the tunnel. "If you guys want to go back, do it. Don't hesitate. You're young, keep that in mind."

Behind their water-streaked polycarbonate face shields they looked like boys, frightened little boys. They looked at each other, then at Kenney.

Iversen said, "We're going with you."

Yeah," St. Aubin said, a little more hesitantly.

Kenney j looked them over and knew they were scared because he was scared, but they could never admit it. Their youth had pride, macho pride. A man was like that before he saw fifty, before he saw the tunnel of his own life narrowing before him. These two puffed-out their chests and inflated their balls and told themselves nothing could touch them because their youth would protect them. They would never admit to fear. Unlike Kenney himself who readily admitted fear and knew he was seriously fucked here, but pushed on out of sheer curiosity now, morbid curiosity. If this place was intent on killing him, then he would know its secrets first, he would see things no man had and lived to tell the tale.

It was odd, but there was comfort in that.

He got on his handpack and checked in with Godfrey, knowing the units on the surface were monitoring everything.

On they went.

St. Aubin came up with the idea of duct-taping their flashlights to the riot guns and it was a smart idea. That way you could keep both hands on your rifle and still see everything there was to see.

They moved on and the water got deeper and came up to their bellies and seemed to get blacker. Whatever it was they'd come to see, it was close now. More remains bobbed in the water, but there were worse things than the dead and they all knew it. Their lights reflected off the polluted waste they marched through and danced over the crumbling brick walls like spotlights. Their splashing sounds echoed through the passage.

They saw more of the fungus, if that's what it was. Good God, the passage walls were threaded with it like some elaborate vein networking. Whatever this was all about down here, the fungus was part and parcel of it and maybe everything they had seen and would yet see were but extensions of it.

It was food for thought.

"Listen," Kenney said, freezing up. There had been a sound ahead, a big sound. But now it was gone. He shook his head. "Nothing."

But it wasn't nothing because none of them were moving now. They waited, they tensed, they listened. It seemed that the water was filled with odd, half-glimpsed shapes now.

Maybe it was their imagination.

But probably not.

The brickwork had mostly fallen away the further they went, and the walls were earthen, muddy, dropping away in chunks now. Water ran in streams from networks of reaching tree roots that dangled above. They began to bump into things in the murk, things lying beneath the surface. St. Aubin went on his ass once. They had to move carefully.

Kenney knew what those things were—long, wooden boxes, but he wasn't saying and didn't until dozens of them started sprouting from the water like tree stumps: coffins. Most were lidless, splintered, scathed with what could only be claw marks and worm holes. Their satin linings were hanging out like viscera, faded and speckled with mildew when they were evident at all. Most of them had been gutted and shredded. They found no remains in any of them.

"A cemetery," Iversen said in a high, whining voice. "That's what this place is, a fucking cemetery."

Kenney could just imagine how the things of Clavitt Fields had tunneled through the darkness, coming up beneath that cemetery across the road from the farmhouse, pulling caskets down into their lair. It was appalling, really, but made perfect sense.

The water was scummy with bits of human anatomy—rank tissue and decayed flesh like a skim of fat. More islands of fungus appeared. It seemed to be growing right out of the coffins. They splashed ahead, trudged awkwardly. The floor of the tunnel was uneven now, lumpy and twisting and heaved-up, full of holes and things that felt like boulders and sticks beneath their boots but were not boulders and sticks at all.

They had to go back. Kenney knew this now.

Everyone was trembling at the edge of lunacy. Go back and dynamite this entire mess, that was the thing to do.

St. Aubin screamed.

He spun in a wild circle and opened up with his riot gun. And then everyone was shooting and stumbling through the water and it took a moment for Kenney to see them—the *things*.

The descendants of the original, depraved inhabitants of Clavitt Fields.

They were coming up out of the water and attacking now. In the arcing, glancing illumination of the flashlights, he could see very little. Just hunched, emaciated figures knitted with a colorless, rolling flesh the color of bacon grease that hung in sheets from their frames like moldering, crawling blankets. He caught glimpses of faces riddled with innumerable holes and rents, others covered in cauls and braided excrescences that seemed to wriggle like flatworms.

One of them rocketed out of the filth, its face twisted into a bubbling, fungal mask and Kenney pulled the trigger, blowing it in half. He kept shooting and so did the others, but it was hopeless. They were in a nest of them and there was no advance, no retreat. Four or five of them emerged from the water like wriggling worms, boneless things with fungoid flesh and tumescent faces and eyeballs only a shade whiter than their mottled complexions and oily locks.

Iversen screamed as they squirmed over him and dragged him down.

St. Aubin was whimpering and crying and yelling. He stumbled into Kenney and Kenney shoved him aside and began firing again, repulsed at how the buckshot made those things literally explode.

Then hands as cold as dry ice and covered with a chill, quivering flesh were at his throat. He brought the butt of the shotgun back and felt it smash into something that yelped and slid away in the water. Another came up right in front of him. Its face was slack and rubbery, the nose collapsed into a skullish cavern.

It was all bad, of course, but what was even worse was a sluggish liquid flow of some pale yeasty material that came out of its eyes in gurgling clots and engulfed its face like it was trying to eat it.

It hissed at him like a cockroach, the spawn of witches. Its lips were nearly fused together by tiny hairlike filaments of mold.

Skeletal, knobby hands took hold of the riotgun…then it was yanked from his oily gloves and he was alone, only St. Aubin's light behind him, bobbing and swaying as he splashed away into the distance.

Kenney ran towards him, knocking three of them out of the way and then a fourth exploded into his path and he instinctively struck out at it. His fist sank through its belly, through tissue and organ which had the spongy consistency of wet bread. It went right through the thing as if it was made of jelly. With a shrill, maddened cry, he pulled his hand back, felt it graze rubbery bones and then the thing fell away only to be replaced by another with a head like a nodding fleshy balloon.

He could hear them coming after him, but he kept running, stumbling through the water until he found St. Aubin pressed up against a wall, moaning and whimpering. He'd stripped away his mask and was sucking in lungfuls of that corrupt, dank air. His face was wet with sweat.

Kenney took hold of him and saw he was a wreck, that he was beyond words, so he took his gun from him and—

And fell backward, screaming into that carrion soup…because he saw what was behind the deputy. The walls were punched with a series of tunnels, small ones you would have had to crawl through on your belly. Like the honeycombs of a bumblebee's nest.

And the scream barely left his lips when a tangle of white arms covered in some shivering gelatinous secretion reached from the hole behind St. Aubin and pulled him bodily into the opening. His screams faded into the distance.

And then Kenney was alone as they came from behind him and others began to slither from those holes with smooth, snakelike undulations.

32

Iversen broke free of a mutiny of clutching, clawing hands and surfaced, battering at the mutant things with his riotgun. He was out of shot but he brandished it like a club. One of them rose up before him and he smashed it in the face with the butt and it literally came apart, spraying over the surface of the water.

Go, go, go, get away, get away.

These were the words that echoed in his head, and he did not try to reason or make sense of any of it. This was survival, fight or flight and he had to get free of this awful place.

He stumbled blindly up passages, turning into others that looked safe until he found himself in a tunnel with slick, earthen walls, the filthy water up to his waist. In his panic, he was not sure where he had gone or where he was now.

With trembling fingers, he stripped his mask off. "KENNEY!" he shouted. "ST. AUBIN! JESUS CHRIST, SOMEBODY ANSWER ME!"

But all he heard was his own voice echoing out into the darkness.

Thank God his flashlight was still working. He stabbed his beam of light up the tunnel and down the way he had come. He saw nothing but dripping walls, clots of clay dropping into the water now and again. A stagnant mist rose from the soup in lacey tendrils. Without the mask on, the stink was horrendous. Not just rot and decay and stagnant water, but a sharp odor of methane and seeping gases.

He fumbled his handpack radio and tried to get a channel but it was ruined from being submerged. He tossed it aside. He had half a dozen shells in his bag. He fed them into the riotgun and tried to think calmly, reasonably, but the idea of that, of course, was simply out of the question.

In the distance, he thought he heard a muted splashing sound.

He waited, listening intently.

Nothing.

You have to think carefully now, a voice in the back of his head told him. *It has never been so important as it is now. Think. Reason. Kenney and St. Aubin are probably fucking dead and maybe Godfrey and the others are, too. You have to proceed like they are. You have to backtrack and fight your way out of here.*

Yes, that's exactly what he needed to do, but the idea of moving, of making noise and drawing those things to him was unthinkable. There was no choice, though. He waited a few more minutes, listening not only for the things but a sound that would tell him he was not alone down there because that was the greatest horror of all: being trapped alone in this flooded tomb.

Move.

He started inching his way back down the passage. He came to where they split and tried to remember which one he had come from. Christ, it was hard to be sure. It must have been the left one, though. Yes, it had to be. If he followed that one down it would lead into the main passage where he had been attacked. Or had there been another tunnel?

No, no, no! Jesus Christ, don't second guess yourself!

He started moving down the passage, only there was really no way to know if he was going in the right direction or not. Everything looked the same and in his panicked flight he had not taken the time to notice any details. He moved deeper into the passage. The farther he went, the more he became certain that it was not the right one at all. He didn't remember the walls being so narrow. And the water was getting deeper, the mist more dense.

This wasn't right at all.

The smell of dank rot filled his head. He felt giddy.

The gases, you idiot. The gases.

He pulled the mask back on and his head cleared after a few moments. He was in the wrong passage. He would have to go back…yet, he wasn't sure if that was the right course of action or not. His light showed him that the passage widened considerably just ahead. In his flashlight beam, he could see that the mist was moving in that direction which told him that there might be an opening to the surface up there somewhere that was sucking the mist up and out.

He moved forward carefully.

The water went down gradually until it was slopping around his ankles. He came to another set of passages. There were three of them this time. His light showed him that one was basically a crawlspace; the other sloped down in the distance as if it might be caved-in. He chose the third. The mist was being pulled into it. He would follow it for a bit and if he saw nothing promising, he would back track and take his chances in the main passage.

If you can find it, dummy. You keep taking different tunnels and you'll be chasing your own tail in no time. Ten years from now someone will find your yellowed bones.

No, Iversen decided that was not going to happen.

He liked this new passage. It was essentially no different from the others—save muddy walls and dripping ceiling and abundant foulness—save that the mist was moving faster now in his flashlight beam. He was getting close to the source and he could feel the sweet touch of freedom reaching out for him. Maybe it was all in his head, but he honestly did not think so.

He was going to fucking do this.

The passage widened, and he ducked under some gnarled tree roots—and his feet went out from beneath him. The floor suddenly canted downward at a 45° angle like a kid's slide and then he was on his ass sliding down a forking, nearly triangular tunnel with more twists and turns in it than the ductwork of an old building. He slid with gathering speed, bumping against walls and hydroplaning first on his back then his belly until he finally splashed into the mother of all mud puddles.

He came up with a cry, pawing clay from his face and spitting out mud.

The puddle was up to his waist, a turgid, slimy pool of drainage that bobbed with floating mats of fungi and bloated rats that were feverish with flies. The buzzing was so loud he could barely hear himself think. Slime dripped from the walls and water trickled from the ceiling in a ceaseless flow that sounded like a dozen men pissing simultaneously. The chamber reached as far as his light could see. After three or four abortive attempts at trying to crawl back up the passage, he resigned himself to the fact that he was seriously screwed here.

He was trapped.

His only hope was that rescue got to him before the things did.

Knowing this, watching his flashlight beam steadily dimming, Iversen began to sob deep in his throat as the darkness pressed in closer.

33

As Kenney and the others first encountered the inhabitants of the underworld, Sheriff Godfrey, Beck, and Chipney entered a flooded cavern.

The tunnel they followed had opened now into a huge, natural chamber where the water washed around their chests. It was about twenty feet wide, but less than seven in height. Had they been any taller, their heads would have brushed the muddy, rocky ceiling.

The sheriff knew it was getting too deep.

Just like he knew this was all pretty hopeless and that he should take these men up and out of there, come back with a properly equipped demo team and blow this place…but he couldn't. He'd put a call into above said, yeah, everything was fine, fine, but it was a lie and he knew it. He'd seen so much now that had withered his soul, but he needed more. He needed to actually *see* them.

And then he did.

A half dozen of them rose from the water gradually as if they were being lifted from below and he saw, he finally saw what had haunted Bellac Road for so very long.

And, Jesus, just like Pearl...or the thing pretending to be Pearl.

Leprous and blotched, pale as parchment, their distorted and sunless faces were cut by agonized grins and sunk with glistening, sightless eyes like graveyard pits. Their hair was long and white and threaded with filth, hanging over their features in greasy, wet braids. They had flesh like cooled, puddled candle wax. It barely covered the skeletons below—ribs burst forth and cheekbones thrust from faces and orbits jutted obscenely and everywhere, he could see their bones. And the flesh itself...more like rotting garments, it hung and pulsed and dangled in fearsome loops and strands. Veils of it trailed out around them, floating like grim bridle trains.

They surged forward, and the deputies started shooting. Gnarled hands reached out for them. Someone screamed. The water boiled around them. Lights were flashing and jumping, and on they came, those grisly faces coming out of the misting darkness like cloven spookshow skulls.

Godfrey and his deputies were stumbling away, shooting and shooting, except Chipney was gone, and there was no hope of saving him or even knowing where he was. The lights bounced with each explosion of the riot guns and Godfrey caught a sight that turned his mind to sauce—dozens of them wriggling and crawling and creeping like maggots on roadkill.

And then they disappeared.

In no hurry, they sank below the surface and the water bubbled and went still, strands of sloughed skin drifting like confetti.

Godfrey and Beck charged through the chest high swamp, but it was slow going and they knew they didn't stand a chance. They fought through shivering nets of fungus that were warm and greasy. But they would not give in, not yet. And then, just ahead, a cavern mouth opened above the waterline. They pulled themselves up and in, and it was dry in there. Rubble and debris covered the rocky floor, and water stood in slimy puddles, but, Jesus, for all that it was dry, dry.

They had barely made it in there, wildly stripping off their masks, not caring about the smell anymore, when a profusion of clown-white hands erupted from the slimy water and began to drag themselves up.

They ran, stumbling in their waterlogged waders, and the cavern narrowed, widened, narrowed again. The sloping ceiling forced them down to their hands and knees and then spit them out in a grotto that was huge and wide and squeaking with countless rats. Before them was a wall. A wall easily thirty feet high and twice that wide. A wall built completely of bones. Skulls and femurs and tibias and scapulas all arranged with an exacting precision that was frightening. It was like some kind of shrine and Godfrey wondered crazily what sort of minds could conceive of something like that.

But then he was at it, tearing and clawing and digging through the masonry of human bones that were pitted and yellow with age. They came apart in his fingers like ancient vases and desert-dried pottery and there was a rumbling as the entire wall collapsed like a house of cards and bones rained down on him.

And on the other side was a den of the things, all of them shrieking and squealing and flaking apart, all creeping in his direction on their hands and knees like a migration of human insects and he was buried alive in their blubbery, clawing bodies.

Beck hid beneath the wall of bones that had rained down on him, finding safety and camouflage in the depths of the ossuary, hiding and trembling like a hunted rodent. He did not move. He barely breathed. A twisted voice in his head told him he could wait there for as long as it took, that he would be safe and those things would never, ever find him.

But he was wrong.

As he listened, they began to dig their way towards him, whispering and grunting and chattering their teeth. Slowly, bone by bone, he was being unearthed, his secret lair exposed. It wasn't until their fingers brushed over him that he began to scream.

34

Searching along the slick clay walls with his dying flashlight, Iversen nearly forgot about the extra D batteries tucked into the pockets of his tactical vest. He dug them out frantically and succeeded in dropping one of them into the muddy water. *Shit!* He groped blindly about for it and was certain that he would never find it because that's how things worked in desperate, horrible, and nightmarish situations like this.

Irony.

Yes, that was the word. It was how Fate or God or Destiny took the wind out of your sails, how it leveled the playing field and showed you just how lucky you'd been in all things and how you would be lucky no more.

He nearly started laughing at one point because in some deranged, heartbreaking, purely fucked-up sort of way, it *was* funny. Then his fingers found the cylinder of the battery and wiped the muddy goo off it. He unzipped his tac vest, and used what dry spots he could find to get the last moisture off it.

Okay. Good.

Do what has to be done.

He fumbled out the used up batteries in the pitch blackness and inserted the new ones. He did this as carefully as he could under the circumstances, not daring to drop any of them. He held them so tightly his fingertips practically left indentations in them.

He clicked on the light.

It was steady, but no brighter which meant it wasn't the batteries at all but the flashlight itself. It was supposed to be waterproof. In fact, it was guaranteed to be 100% waterproof. So it was either a manufacturing defect or it had been damaged somehow, maybe in his falling slide, and water had leaked in.

There was no time to consider it.

His face beaded with sweat, Iversen pulled the mask back so he could see better and started working his way around the walls of the chamber looking for an opening. The idea that he would find one seemed absurd even to him, but he did find a passage. Just the one. A low and narrow crawlspace, but it was better than nothing. He took it.

He crawled along on his hands and knees through the sodden tunnel, his shoulders brushing the walls and the top of his mask scraping along the ceiling. He was not claustrophobic by nature, yet he could very much feel the walls closing in. Loose globs of runny clay dropped down on the back of his neck, water trickled down his face. The stink of subterranean decay was almost overpowering.

He paused more than once thinking he heard something, but it must have been his own sounds reverberating. The tunnel twisted and turned, but thankfully went no deeper into the earth. In fact, it seemed to be steadily ascending, so he was going up to…something.

He stopped.

Listen.

His skin crawling in tight waves, he heard something. It was a low, distant murmuring coming up the tunnel from behind him. Try as he might, he could not be sure what it was. He began to crawl faster and faster until sweat stung his eyes and his breath scratched in his throat. Then the passage opened, and he dropped into a flooded bowl with no egress. All that fucking work and he was at a dead end.

He wanted to laugh again.

But he didn't dare.

He heard no more sounds and that was good because he had no choice: he had to go back. He forced himself back into the tunnel and the going was much easier because he was slowly moving downwards. After a time, he saw the opening and a voice in his mind said, *nothing ventured, nothing gained*, and he almost laughed at that…then there was a sharp, stabbing pain at the back of his neck.

A tree root?

No, there hadn't been any before; he was sure of it.

He started moving towards the opening and something brushed against his back. He squirmed, rolling over, nearly becoming wedged in the passage, getting a face full of wet clay in the process. He could not bring the flashlight back around, but he sensed rather than saw movement.

Gripped by a suffocating fright, he clawed his way out of the opening and dropped back into the chamber. It was big in there and that was its only saving grace. The brown water slopped back and forth in lazy waves, the sound of it echoing and echoing.

The fear did not lessen, it increased.

There was something in the water with him.

He saw a humped form out of the corner of his eye and then another. Panic breaking in him, he started firing blindly at things real and things imagined and then he was out of shot. Something brushed his leg and something else brushed against his back. He let out a low, echoing cry. He swung the light around in every direction, creating echoing splashing sounds and slimy waves of muck that broke against him.

As he brought the light around again, he glimpsed a distorted face rising from the murk.

Then it was gone.

He fell back into the water and yanked himself up and something latched onto the back of his neck. He reached back there and his fingers sank into cold, gelatinous tissue with no more substance than the moist clay of the passages. Shrieking, he tore at it, strips of flesh coming apart in his fingers and a warm juice spraying over the back of his hand. Whatever it was, it cried like a squealing human infant.

He was hit from the left.

He kicked out at it, spraying water against the wall…and something white like a pair of tiny doll hands grabbed the shotgun and yanked it from his sweaty fingers and pulled it under. The light died and the dark rushed in. Things moved around him. He could hear their clogged breathing.

The flares.

He grabbed one from his tac vest and twisted the cap. Flickering red-hued light filled the chamber, making everything seem to bob and weave. He saw the things in the water with him. They looked very much like fetuses from freakshow jars…bulbous-headed, limbs spindly and tiny fingers set with black claws. Their eyes were like blank white bubbles, their flesh the color and consistency of pork chop fat, but weirdly translucent and set with networks of purple and black veins, some of which were thick as worms.

Iversen put the flare in their direction and they backed away, but others rose up behind him. He kept turning this way and that, jabbing the flare at distorted fetal faces, but each time they were closer, and each time there were more of them. Then they leaped and six or seven were hanging from him, placing suckering mouths against his bare arms, his neck, and face. They were blubbery and flaccid things like newborn maggots.

One of them bit into his wrist and he dropped the flare. He tore and beat at them, feeling them coming apart under his fists, but there were always more and they fastened themselves to him like blood-swollen ticks.

He screamed as their little fingers dug into him, as nubby teeth pierced his skin. He cried out in agony as their talons sheared his face from the bone beneath and he choked on his own blood. Before he sank into the pool of thrashing water, he felt one of them jump on his head and sink fangs like ice tongs through his skull and into his brain.

35

Kenney wasn't sure where he was. The mutants—because that's what they were—seemed to come in waves and he emptied his riotgun into advancing hordes of them, just managing to stay free of their clutching fingers.

He tried his handpack radio again and again, but all he was getting now was static. The mutants had been corralling him, he realized. It seemed insane, but that's exactly what they were doing. Attacking from every side, pushing him into side passages and low, sloping tunnels and doing it to get him more confused and more lost.

Maybe they're not human, but they sure as hell are smart.

Trying to keep from panicking, hoping that Hyder would send a relief party down when he could not be reached, Kenney entered another chamber that was huge and echoing. The walls were made of fungus, draperies of the stuff, greasy and pink and pulsating. It trailed into the water and hung in loops from the ceiling overhead.

That's when he saw a figure come splashing in his direction.

He brought up his riotgun and only hesitated from firing when a light found him and he heard a voice crying out, "KENNEY! KENNEY! DON'T SHOOT! DON'T SHOOT!"

It was Beck.

He was torn up pretty good. He still had his riotgun, but his gas mask was gone, his tac vest and waders torn, his face scratched with bleeding rents. "They came from everywhere…they got Godfrey…I barely got away." He leaned up against Kenney. "I barely got away."

Kenney nodded. "They got St. Aubin. I don't know about Iversen. Right now, we have to worry about ourselves and get the hell out of here. How many rounds you got?"

"Five or six. No more."

"I only have a couple myself. Let's go."

They moved on into the tunnel Kenney had come out of. They had to find that main passage, he knew, or they could wander down here for weeks. It was a fucking labyrinth, and he didn't want to think about how far it went on for.

The tunnel snaked this way and that, the water coming up past their hips now. It was slow and viscous, equal parts clay and water and slime. They were tense, anxious.

A ripple passed through the muck.

"Hold it," Beck said, shining his light around, the ripples fading away. "Something…there's something in the water, something in the water with us."

And he was right.

Whatever it was, maybe it knew the game was up for it erupted from the putrid, brown water like a monstrous worm. It hit Beck and took him down before he could even think of firing. In the arc of his flashlight, it looked reptilian, boneless, a fluid and pulsing thing.

Kenney stumbled back and fell, coming up just in time to see Beck burst from the water, spraying mud from his mouth.

Something was on his back, riding him—a mutant that was fat and heaving like a slug. Its mouth was at his throat making obscene sucking sounds. He screamed and fell back into the muck.

Kenney didn't waste a second.

He reached in there and took hold of something oily, something slippery and bloated, yanked on it with all his strength until it came up and twisted around, hitting him hard. He fell against the wall, a brown and muddy thing making first a shrill bleating sound, then a squealing like a pissed-off hog. He could see its mouth snapping at him, blunt teeth wanting to dig into his face. He had a tight grip on its throat and he wasn't letting go. The creature, he realized, was a woman of sorts but misshapen and hideously deformed. Her hands were like huge, flattened spades, the individual fingers webbed together. There was a row of pulsating sacs down her torso like pendulous teats. They swayed like water balloons as she writhed and fought and tore into him. Her back and head were covered in short, rubbery bristles and her mouth was a piglike snout exhaled hot, fetid air in his face.

She was incredibly strong, forcing Kenney deep into the slop. He screamed and raged, something in him refusing the idea of death…and then there was a resounding explosion and the pig-woman was blown free of him.

Beck, bloody but unbowed, stood there with his riotgun. He had stuck the barrel of it right up to the pig-woman's side and pulled the trigger.

The pig woman herself…or *itself*…was roiling in the mud, her blood swirling in with the brown and yellow muck. Her guts were hanging out, bleached and distended like jellyfish washed up on a beach. They trailed behind her as she tried to crawl away.

When she died, she simply sank like a log in quicksand.

Kenney was out of breath, his muscles aching, his head full of a shrieking white noise. The pig-woman's spade hands had torn through his coat and shirt, ripping bleeding gashes into his belly and chest.

He turned to Beck. "I owe you one," he said.

36

They had Godfrey right where they wanted him and he knew it.

He'd fought free of them for a time but they had him cornered now and he realized with a sinking feeling in his chest that he'd only gotten away because they'd allowed him to. He'd been backing away from them deeper into the tunnels and now he was in some kind of cocoon of fungi. It was like a pocket of the stuff. There was no way out. The mutants were ringed around the opening, just waiting, just watching for what would happen next. They grinned with pulpy faces, making whispering sounds.

The fungi cocoon was vaguely pulsating and to Godfrey it felt like the beat of some great heart.

Yes, because this isn't some accidental mutation, it's on purpose. You're in a womb of the stuff.

He realized then the relationship between the fungus and the descendants of Clavitt Fields. They had merged and become one. Elena had it right, at least some of it. She told them a very, very old story of a meteorite falling from the sky—*a huge flaming stone...a piece of star...fell from the sky many centuries ago*—and burying itself in the earth and how the people of Clavitt Fields had biologically degenerated, becoming these things he was looking upon now. He remembered Kenney mentioning radiation, and that seemed a good, if farfetched bet at the time. And maybe there *was* radioactivity involved, but it was more than that because there had been something living in that piece of falling star, something that crawled down into the ground and blighted the entire area, maybe gradually remaking the inhabitants of Clavitt Fields into things more like itself. Elena had spoken of some old drunk many years ago seeing something made of eyes and crawling lights coming out of the Ezren well, something that blinded him permanently just looking on it.

It was still here.

It still lived.

The mutants were part of it, they had achieved some morbid symbiosis with it.

And Godfrey was trapped not in a cocoon of fungi, but in a cocoon of its flesh…this entire underworld was infested by the thing.

And these were the revelations that occurred to him in his final moments as he looked the gorgon in the face and prepared for his end.

The pink cocoon was much like the mutants themselves, made of some gelid, spongy material, but while they were bleached and bloodless things in some advanced stage of abiotrophic decline, the cocoon itself was pink and juicy and unnaturally healthy. He could see an elaborate system of veins or arteries branching out just beneath its surface. It was sticky and unpleasant and he knew if he stayed in one position long, he would be glued to it.

It began to move.

The mutants began to murmur excitedly.

It began to move around him, vibrating and pulsing. Tiny flaccid ripples passed through its mass as it seemed to contract and expand in peristaltic waves. That's what Godfrey felt right before it began consuming him, right before it put out tiny wire-thin filaments that were blood-red and glistening and he shrieked in agony as they crawled up his pantlegs and punctured his skin, sliding beneath his fingernails and entering his ass and sliding up the shaft of his penis and drilling in through his navel. Within seconds, he was securely webbed and securely impaled, a thrashing figure whose screaming mouth ejected a mist of blood.

The thing had him and it was ingesting him.

His flesh began to liquefy, his face coming apart in dripping ribbons, oozing from the skull beneath like snot. Now it was not just those filaments working on him, but creepers of gray jelly big around as thumbs. They emerged from the cocoon mass, coiling and constricting and pushing their way beneath his dissolving skin and he continued to scream, his mouth dripping now like hot tallow.

He was barely human by that point, a writhing and animate puppet rooted to the cocoon. He was wound in creepers. They fed from his eyes and mouth and fingertips. With one last burst of strength and survival instinct, he tried to fight free, and it sounded like weeds being pulled from the earth.

The cocoon let out a high, piping cry.

Great white rootlets pierced him now, pulling him back down into the fleshy bed of his own biologic ruin.

He was human in form only, the alien tissue owning him, snaking and wriggling within and without him. Every time the hole of his mouth attempted to open, jellied tendrils spread from it in a blossoming congestion like rootlets of woodrot. White and looping fingers of fungi undulated like whips from

his fingertips, tasting the air and seeking new flesh to despoil, which was only his own.
   This was communion with the Mother Organism.
   And the most appalling part of it was that he was not dead.

37

Chipney had been dragged off into the depths, deposited here in this womb of fungus that seemed to breathe around him with barely audible susurrations. When he opened his eyes, he was sluggish and tired as if he had just consumed a huge meal. And, oddly, he felt that way—overfed. But that was insane because he had not eaten. He had been dumped here and lost consciousness. He had vague recollections of one dream piled on top of another, all of them so weirdly hallucinogenic and surreal they were almost psychedelic.

The last time he had dreamed with such organic vibrancy was when he had taken Chantix to quit smoking five years before. He had woken each morning feeling exhausted as if he had run a marathon or plowed through *War and Peace* in a single sitting. The only other time he had experienced anything remotely similar was when he had dropped acid in college.

It's the gases down here, it must be the gases, he told himself with a sleepy voice that fumbled over the words, *they're making you loopy.*

The good thing was, he was alone.

Absolutely alone.

The mutant things had left.

His riotgun was gone, of course, and he had no light to see by, but he could remember the way he had been brought into this place. God, the floor, the walls…living tissue. It was disgusting. He felt around for the passage and was amazed when he found it in the darkness.

Keep moving, keep going. Let your instincts get you out of here. It's all you have now.

The tunnel was set with countless passageways and channels and, though he was completely lost, he listened an internal voice that told him to keep moving up and up, and whenever he found an opening above, he did just that.

He was crawling through an extremely cramped, dripping tunnel now that seemed to be collapsing in sodden heaps of muck. There were things above him that he kept bumping his head into, hard things, and his fingers more than once explored them and found them to be made of rotting wood. But it meant nothing to him, not the undersides of slabs he encountered or the swollen tree roots he fought through. Nor even the other things he began to find, things which could be nothing other than mushy, bloated corpses that he clawed his way over and through, fingers digging ruts in ruined faces and valleys in jellied abdomens.

The stench was black and odious, an invasive aura that wound him and held him in fingers of putrefaction.

But he refused to think about it or even acknowledge it. That stuff was for later. Now there was just survival, and it was enough.

He worked and slid like an eel through rot and decay and then his fingers were reaching into empty air. He propelled himself forward and landed hard on a stone floor that was wet and cold. But smooth, even.

Concrete?

He pulled himself through puddles and began frantically digging in his waders, beneath to his shirt pocket where he kept his cigarettes, his lighter.

He hadn't dared light it before...all those gases...but now in this wide open space, why not?

Sanity began to seep back into his mind now that there was the possibility of escape. His lighter was wet, and it took a few moments of striking the wheel until finally it began to spark out of sheer friction and dry itself and then, yes, a flame, bright, blinding, a million suns exploding before him.

He opened his eyes into slits and saw.

He was in a mausoleum, a burial vault. The sweating stone walls were set with funerary inscriptions and black cavities into which caskets could be pushed. But they had been torn from their sepulchral berths and scattered over the floor, shattered, their contents taken away. Everywhere there were splinters of wood and tarnished brass handles, shattered lids and shredded streamers of casket silk like party confetti...but no bones.

Not a single set of remains.

Except for what was laid across the framework of a bier. He saw the brown uniform, the badge, the yellow department logo and knew it was Riegan...Riegan who'd disappeared out in the field that night.

He was being tenderized in this wormy, palpable dampness.

Chipney found a set of steps and clawed up them. They were covered with a spongy yellow moss. Before him was a rusted metal door, and he beat his fists against it until they were raw and bleeding, then the lighter burned his fingers and went out.

I'm this close, you idiots! Get me out of here! Don't let me die now!

"Not now," he said under his breath. "Oh dear God, not now…"

Then below, the sound of motion, of creeping and rustling as the things swarmed through the hole and into the crypt, filling it with their ravenous, fleshy forms.

38

"There's movement up ahead," Kenney said as he waded through the filthy waters with Beck. "I thought I saw something."

Beck hadn't seen it. All he cared about was getting out and nothing else seemed to matter. He was ready to kill anything or anyone that got in the way of that. They were in the main passage now and if things worked out, they could be to the ladder in fifteen minutes or less. This drove him and it was enough.

He saw a ripple in the murky slop and slowed a bit.

He tasted a sour sweetness in his mouth. Was that the taste of fear? Of adrenaline? A mixture of both? He didn't know. He pushed forward with a bravado and a confidence that even surprised him.

I'm getting the fuck out of here and that's all there is to it. I won't take no for an answer.

This was like some kind of mantra playing in his head.

Behind him, Kenney tried the radio again with no luck. Soon, maybe, they were bound to pick up something. He told himself this, amazed at his own optimism.

And then hell broke loose.

He saw the folly of being hopeful.

A half a dozen of the mutants came vaulting out of the water, dragging their sloughing skins behind them. With a broken cry, Beck started shooting, blasting away wildly. He used up all his shot within seconds and he could not even be sure he had hit any of them. The riotgun was slapped from his hands by a woman who wore her flesh like a badly fitting garment. It was a tarp that flowed around her.

She reached for him with gnarled hands like twisted tree roots, black talons streaking at his eyes.

She barely missed him. He struck out and felt his fist sink into spongy tissue, making him stumble backwards with revulsion. He nearly went into the muddy water, but she caught him and wouldn't let him go.

He heard Kenney shouting as he blasted away, but little else.

One of her clawed hands stabbed forward, ripping his larynx out, and with such force it dislodged the muscles in his neck and dislocated his jaw in one fell swoop. He shrieked, but she slapped a gummy hand over his mouth and he gagged on the juice that squeezed from it.

Kenney couldn't help him.

He was batting them away with his riotgun, trying to beat a hasty retreat to get out of harm's way. In the strobing light, he thought he saw two or three of them seize Beck and tear him quite neatly in half like a paper doll.

39

St. Aubin was not dead. Maybe not truly alive anymore in the normal sense of the word, but he was certainly not dead. His mind was a trembling, yellow thing that skulked and shivered in the dim corners of his brain. Now and then sanity would rear its head and tell him in no uncertain terms the levels of madness and horror he had sunk to, but mostly he kept it locked away in a musty trunk.

But he was still a man and still had a sense of identity, even though he had trouble remembering exactly who he was or how he'd come to be in this predicament. He subsisted mostly on the raw, rough gruel of instinct. It was this that fed and filled him, kept his limbs moving and his mind focused and resilient. If it wasn't for this atavistic drive, he would long ago have drawn into himself and slammed the door shut.

He was crawling through sloping, narrow tunnels on his belly. Tunnels so small and cramped that the sides brushed his shoulders and the roof brushed the top of his head. Caked with filth, he crawled on and on through that black, sucking mud. Like some insane mole, he was quite blind now in the absolute darkness and moved only by feel, his fingers constantly searching and divining the suffocating dimensions ahead.

Part of his brain remembered, but his conscious mind kept these memories buried.

It was important not to recall certain things.

Like those grubby, fleshy hands that had pulled him away from Kenney and dragged him down that endless, meandering tangle of pest holes, finally depositing him in some profane den where still more hands accepted him and noses sniffed him and fingers explored him. He could remember this part very well, for the uneven walls were lit by a dim illumination that radiated from what appeared to be a peculiar blue-green mold imbued with some weird bioluminescence. He could not see clearly, but well enough as in twilight or pale moonlight.

That's when he began to put things together.

They thought he was dead.

They had tucked him into a tight, cloistered cell that had been dug out of the slick, dripping clay walls. And as they did this (and he let them do it, God yes, paralyzed both physically and emotionally with terror), he saw other forms pressed into countless other cells. And knew, despite the grainy light, that those tangled, knotted things were the bodies of men and women that had been stuffed into holes so they could soften to pulp, and decay properly before being eaten.

And he was just another one.

Yes, yes, the food is the flesh and the corpse is the meat, the blood is the wine and the unplucked, untasted cadaver is the bread to be broken by grisly hands to stuff in the mouths of ravenous ghouls. It all fits and it all works and it all makes a beautiful sort of sense, doesn't it? Well...DOESN'T IT?

And, God, but it did, oh sweet Jesus in your lofty throne high above the charnel pits far below, it made perfect sense. Not men and women down here. Oh, no, no, no, no, perish the fucking thought, friends and neighbors. These were not men nor women nor humans exactly, just…just…obscene/debased/degenerate things that cannot walk in the light but must creep in the tomblike darkness. Worms, human maggots that feast upon the dead, sharpening their claws on coffin lids and their teeth on pitted bones.

And if you're happy and you know it, clap your hands and no one laughs when the hearse goes by…hee, hee, haw, haw.

His mind swam in and out of this self-perpetuating sea of dementia. He recalled waking and seeing that the others had left and there was only some ancient, stick-thin creature in attendance. It looked to be a woman, incredibly old, her face invisible beneath a mop of dun, colorless hair woven with sticks and clods of dirt. Her chest was writhing with some horrible podia like teats on a mother hog. She crouched there in the corner, oblivious to all and everything, nibbling at her own fingers. St. Aubin could hear the grinding of her teeth, the wet and abominable sound of her smacking lips and investigative tongue.

And it was bad enough, plenty bad enough being trapped in that hideous lair where human beings were tucked away like fat spiders in a hornet's nest, but it got worse. For there began a bizarre, offensive melody of guttural squealing and yelping sounds. And he saw that the sounds came from the wall directly opposite his own, echoing from countless holes sunk into the clay…and in those holes, squirming, distorted, ghastly things. The old lady dragged herself across the floor and began rending something in a cell directly below St. Aubin's. He heard a wet, pulpy snapping and something like rotting cloth being torn. He was thankful for the gloom, for he couldn't see what she carried and what she fed the things in those grisly holes.

Maybe he couldn't exactly remember his own name, but he knew one thing: He was in a nursery, being seasoned and softened for those appalling and toothless, infantile mouths.

He might have passed out then or crawled into some crack in the floor of his mind where it was dark, cozy, and safe. When he opened his eyes, the mold was shining brightly, revealing something that made his eyes roll in their sockets and his teeth chatter wildly until his gums ached.

That…that…that…what is that I'm seeing? What is that thing that comes out of the darkness?

He could not be sure, only that the sight of it made him piss himself.

There was a thing standing there…well, not exactly standing, but suspended by wires like a marionette, only they were not wires but dozens and dozens and dozens ropy strands of the pink fungal material that infested the subterranean world of the corpse-eaters. And they were not exactly hooked to her—because, oh yes, it was certainly a *her*—but growing into her and out of her, connecting to a huge pink, pulsating mass of morbid tissue that looked quilted, soft and spongy and dripping pearlescent red tears. The strands pulled her, stretched her, flattened her and elongated her, making her into a woman and something quite beyond a woman.

At the sight of it…of her…of *it*, St. Aubin made a sound somewhere between a giggle and a low shrieking.

A stink came off the woman-thing.

It smelled like sour urine and polluted tidal flats and corpses in green ponds.

She's astride a lovely pink web, can't you see that?

Yes, now it was apparent: a glittering pink web that grew within her and without her because she and fungus were one. The webs were strung with shining silken cases, and ruby blood-egg clusters all done up in a finery of feathery tapestries spun from spider-mesh and spider-gauze, a threadwork and maze, a black widow's deadly nest.

Listen, listen...can you hear her? Can you?

There was a scrambling of limbs, a wet sound and a dry sound, a slithering noise and then the sound of fleshy tearing. The woman split open and something repellent bubbled out of her. It was vile and undulant, a pink and creeping horror limned by soft light. It was the fungus, and it poured from her, it gushed and foamed and when its flowing mass retreated back into her...there were something like glistening eggs strung on the strands like beads on a thread.

In his mind, St. Aubin saw that each one held a squirming larva.

In the light, of course, there was no way he could really see this, yet the image was quite vibrant in his mind. He tried to think it away and blink it away, but it remained. And when he looked over at the woman who had sewn herself back up again, she was a globular mass of bleeding eyes.

She was the haunter of the dark.

She was the despoiler of men's minds.

She was a living flux of plastic tissue, of fungus, of woman, a biological machine that reinvented itself with a child's aberrant imagination. It sprouted malformed heads that were huge and bulbous. It became a pale writhing thing like a fetal termite. It threw out a dozen limbs that were not exactly arms or legs and a dozen grasping human hands sprouting chest to crotch like the teats of a cow. Its face became the grotesque, cartoonish saw-toothed grin of a jack-o'-lantern and a veil of gray fungus. Its head mutated into a cluster of blind white eyes and then a semi-human monstrosity that looked like something dumped from a bucket in a dissection room.

She/it/they were slithering and writhing and viscidly alive. Something made of a thousand moving parts...mouths filled with teeth and fingers tipped by claws and tentacles and batwings and accordions of gleaming bone. But for it all, she was still oddly embryonic and unformed. She was forming herself into everything she had encountered in every murky crawlspace and stinking drainage ditch she had crept through, every putrefying corpse and roadkilled animal she stumbled across, every fly and worm and crawling thing that had infested the corpses she fed upon. And much of it was just pure subjective impression.

Regardless, all of it, every bit of it was not intended to frighten him and he knew this. There was an actual agenda behind it all and when he realized it, it was like a ray of light chasing away the darkness in his head.

It's for your benefit, all for your benefit. She's trying to amuse you. She does not want you to be scared. She wants you to be amused so you will not be afraid. Whatever she was and whatever the fungus creature was, they are not hateful creatures.

"But I don't want this," he found himself saying. "I don't want this at all. I want to go…don't you see? I want to go!"

Now she was a thing of glossy pink webs. The great strands and ropes of tissue connected her to the ceiling and walls and even the floor were thickening, replicating themselves until they were a tangled forest, darning and hemming and sewing themselves into mantraps and funnels and nooses. She would stop him. She would knot him up and snare him because she wanted him to stay forever.

Come to me, she said inside his head. *Come to mother. Join me as the others joined me and were remade by me. I'm soft and warm and comforting. Come dream with me.*

St. Aubin could no longer seem to think.

His fingers fumbled around him until his left hand clutched the phallic shape of a mushroom. At first, it felt greasy and foul…then, like velvet. He held it in his hands, the silkiness of it bringing a tactile rapture that made him moan. It felt so wonderful. Somewhere during the process, he brought it up to his mouth and kissed it.

His lips tingled.

It was amazing. It was so soft, so very tender. It was like the cheek of a baby or the down of a chick, both and neither. A bunny's fur felt almost coarse in comparison.

He licked it and it fired his taste buds into new realms that made him tremble and gasp, whimper for more.

He bit into it.

Dear Christ.

It was a rare delicacy, sweet and savory and mouth-watering. It triggered the release of endorphins in his head that flooded his body with a sense of contentment, satisfaction, and pure biochemical joy.

You have eaten me...now enter me.

The sound of her voice made him feel like he was drifting on a lofty, featherbed-soft cloud through a sky of cotton candy. He could not be certain in those dizzying moments whether she came to him or he came to her, he was only aware of *contact*. Of his own hands reaching out to touch her and bisecting her central, webby mass which felt warm and seedy and joyously pulpous like the guts of a pumpkin. That was the ecstasy of it, the tactile delight. He wanted to run his hands through her and swim through her.

And she was only too happy to accept him.

It was like being buried in the cold guts of fish, being sucked into a bog of wriggling entrails. He melted like tallow as he fell into her and there was no pain because unlike Godfrey, he was not frightened of her. She pulsed and purred, coiled and bled pink rivers of tissue until he was engulfed in her depths.

There was a purity to it.

And a beauty beyond words.

40

Chipney had been stumbling through the underground maze for so long now he couldn't be sure where he was.

The creatures had entered the tomb and dragged him back below, down one passage and into another. They could have killed him, but that hadn't seemed to be their primary motivation. It was like they just wanted to keep him down there, good and lost.

But why? What could the possible point of that be?

Somehow, he still clutched the riot gun, but the flashlight was dimming. It wouldn't last long now. The passage he was in twisted and turned, offered endless offshoots and, Jesus, he was moving in circles for all he knew. He had trouble remembering where he was and how it was he had gotten to be there.

He had to dig himself out, but he feared that was impossible now.

This place was a stagnant, compressed, opaque envelope of filth and decay and pestilence. It was all over his skin, in his hair, up his nose, on his tongue, running from his eyes like dirty tears.

But for all that, he could feel a small, weak breeze on him.

So he kept following it, hoping, praying it would lead him out of this madhouse. He could hear rustlings and squeakings and chitterings and now and again a leathery wing brushed his face. Bats. Rats. How harmless they seemed when you were faced with worse things.

Sounds now.

Them? Was it *them?* Had they tracked him down and were, even now, slinking forward to claim him? Was that it?

No, listen, dammit, listen!

Yes, a rushing noise. Like water. Like a waterfall, in fact. Loud and getting louder. Maybe a subterranean river or stream. And maybe, possibly a way out or just a way deeper into this stygian hell.

He began moving quicker through the tunnel now, the water splashing around his ankles. The breeze was much stronger and, Christ, how sweet it indeed smelled. How wonderful. He had forgotten what fresh air felt like against his face, in his lungs, the cool whisk of it against his teeth. It was a joyous thing really, but it only served to amplify the atrophied, stagnant reel of the tunnel system.

He kept moving, the fresh air pulling him along like a thread of hope. Maybe this is why he had seen none of the creatures for so long now. Fresh air and, possibly, sunshine would have been unthinkable to them, abhorrent. They would have avoided it like fumes from a septic tank—unclean, tainted even.

The sound of water was deafening now, and the tunnel was still unwinding before him and when would it ever end? His feet moved faster, his breath rasped in his lungs, his heart pounded fitfully. And the flashlight dimmed and dimmed, began to flicker and, oh, dear Christ, not now, not now! He slapped its cylinder against his leg and it came back brighter and dimmed just as fast. He found that if he kept whacking it against his thigh, it would brighten for a moment or two.

Goddammit!

And then the passage veered off to the right and there was a chamber ahead. The air was still fresh…but he smelled something stale and noisome and, without thinking, he stepped into the chamber…and dropped fifteen feet in a slimy, viscous pool. And all around him, squeaking and rustling and clawing and snapping. He thrashed and fought and pulled himself up out of the festering muck and it smelled just about worse than anything. It was all over his face and down his shirt and up his nose. He still had the riot gun in his hand and the drop had jarred the flashlight and now the beam flickered and exploded with life.

And that's when he saw them—the rats.

With a deathly realization, he looked upon them and they looked upon him. Ranks of them crowding for space in a grim, verminous circle that tightened and tightened. Huge, fat, with greasy pelts and trembling tails, eyes leering with rabies. They were grinding yellowed teeth and making ready.

He started to scream and couldn't stop.

He pulled himself to his feet and realized what he'd fallen into was a collected pool of dung, waste material from the meals of the creatures. A vile, diseased stew of bacteria and filth. A sewer.

He started shooting with his Colt 9mm and got off maybe two rounds that echoed like rolling thunder in the chamber and the rats were in motion. He could never be sure if they were attacking or just stampeding out of fear, but they were everywhere. He could feel their dirty, furry bodies pressing against his legs and their teeth nipping at his waders and feel them clawing at his legs, but by then he was running, stumbling, and he fell into the filth again and little fangs ripped at his face and hands and he kicked and slapped them away.

The flashlight went out for good and a darkness thick as coal dust descended on him.

He plowed drunkenly through the rats, guided only now by sheer instinct that told him to run, run. And he felt the fresh air again and climbed out of that pit and the rats had retreated and, dear God, he probably had rabies. And then he was crawling down another passage on his hands and knees and he saw light. Filmy and gray, but light all the same.

A few pallid fingers of it issuing from a cleft in the rock ahead and he dove straight at it—and then the floor disappeared beneath him and he was falling, falling, end over end towards the sound of rushing water.

41

Kenney's world was chaotic and unbalanced. It was a barrow pit and a madhouse, a hot-blooded nightmare and a subceller freak show. He had escaped the mutants, but they had badly battered him. His head hurt; his face and neck stung from the acidic secretions of their fingers. He was out of rounds for the riotgun, but he held onto it for the flashlight and its effectiveness as a club. He still had his service weapon—a Colt 9mm—and flares. So he was not down and out just yet.

In the darkness, hip deep in the foul brown drainage, he leaned against the wall, unable to go another inch.

Where the fuck is Hyder and those reinforcements? What the hell are they doing up there? He should have sent a rescue team down thirty minutes after we stopped checking in.

Kenney knew he had to remain calm, but with each passing second in that awful place it became harder and harder.

He was lost; he was scared; he was confused. His mind was filled with dusty cobwebs. He was so damn tired he couldn't seem to think straight.

Keep awake. If you do nothing else, keep...awake.

But it wasn't easy. God, no. He was so exhausted from the shock of this entire nightmare and slogging through the stygian depths of the flooded underworld and crawling through cramped tunnels that he could have slept standing up. In fact, he could have gone right out leaning against the warm, mucky wall.

But he wouldn't allow that.

He couldn't allow that.

By sheer force of will he made himself stand erect, chuckling hopelessly deep in his throat when a stream of water warm as piss trickled from above and ran down his cheek. It was followed by a clod of clay that oozed down the bridge of his nose like a melting turd.

He pushed on through the water, refusing to think about the fact that Chipney—Jesus, *Chip*—was probably dead. No marriage. No future. No nothing save a bride left at the altar, crying her eyes out over the cold corpse of her fiancée.

You could have ordered him to stay above.

Yes, that was true, but he was a cop. A damn good cop and that would have been an insult to him, a professional slap in the face from a friend and a colleague and Kenney couldn't do something like that.

Stop thinking and push on.

Yes, that was it.

He followed the tunnel around a bend, noticing that his flashlight beam was flimsy, dimming to a struggling yellow ray that reflected off the swirling gaseous mist rising from the stagnant swamp around him. There was a shelf of rock jutting from the wall just ahead. He would change the batteries there.

That's how tired he was.

So tired he hadn't even noticed the light was going dead. His eyes must have really been beginning to adjust to the murk and that disturbed him.

He made it over to the shelf and it was perfect: a seatlike shelf of limestone. He crawled up onto it, dangled his legs over the edge, and swapped the dying batteries for the fresh ones in his tac vest. God, the light was so bright now it was blinding. He clicked it off, conserving power.

That done, he sat there, listening.

And listening.

He could hear the sound of water dripping, bits of the walls sloughing off, a steady sound of liquid draining into the soup like a leaking pipe. It was nice. It was nearly comforting. It made him feel relaxed. *Too* relaxed, in fact, because his eyes began to drift shut. He didn't bother fighting the exhaustion. He let himself sink into the darkness and raft away on dreams.

Better.

Much better.

He didn't know how long he slept, but he woke to a tugging sensation at his left hand. It was pulling, itching, and generally nagging him. There was a rush of hot, moist, and noisome air blown into his face. The reek was nauseating. It reached yellow fingers down his throat and pulled his stomach up.

He knew what it was.

Even in the darkness, he could see vague shapes clustered around him. Their smell was revolting. He forced himself not to panic. If he did, he knew very well what they could do to him with their claws.

They were hissing.

Smacking their lips.

Ignoring the pain in his left hand, Kenney slowly reached his right hand towards the switch on the flashlight. As he did so, he felt them touching him with hands like soft, warm mittens.

He turned on the light.

The sudden explosion of brilliance made them cry out and cover their faces which were like bloated mushrooms. They backed away, and he pulled a flare from his tac vest, igniting it.

The heat scared them. The light it threw was bright as a welding arc in the darkness. It sent them scurrying, making gobbling and squealing sounds. There had to be a least a dozen of then pulling away like roaches.

Some of them, he saw, were bent over and twisted from the weight of the pink fungus growing on them in slimy mounds. Others were eaten away from it, great chasms where their faces should have been. He saw one with sagging, furry breasts that must have been a woman. She was blown up to grotesque proportions, a pink shivering mass set with yellow spines and draping ribbons of crawling fungi in place of her hair. Her hands were like oven mitts.

Then they were gone.

Kenney sat there, gasping for breath, his throat dry with the spores they had been breathing on him.

He tried to rise from the shelf, but his aching left hand was stuck to the wall…but, no, he saw in the light of the flare and flashlight with a shudder of aversion, that wasn't it at all. Not stuck but tied with strings. Except these strings were mucid and alive, growing right out of the wall like roots and into his hand.

Nearly hysterical at the sight of it, he yanked and pulled with everything he had but the tendrils held tight.

The more strength he put to it, the more it felt like his skin would peel off as if the strings had grown deep into the bones of his hand.

He took the flare and put its burning end on them.

The tendrils tried to pull away from the heat, then crisped and withered and blackened, dropping out of his hand. The others began to push angrily from the wall, coiling and corkscrewing.

Kenney didn't wait around to see what they were going to do. The flare in one hand and the riotgun in the other, he fled.

42

Godfrey was still conscious, not completely, but wavering in the gray netherworld between dream and reality. He was part of the Mother Organism, rooted into her now, yet his mind seemed to drift through her, knowing things and understanding things and somehow maintaining a sort of individuality. Being part of her was a revelation. Her chemistry was utterly alien to what his was used to, so he scaled peaks of euphoria and dropped down into dark abysses. She made adjustments, weaning him slowly and making him part of something much larger than himself, filling him with herself and letting him experience the hallucinatory delight of herself.

The beauty of it was there was no hate or anger.

Those were purely simian reactions to frustrations and disappointments and things that could not be controlled or anticipated. Negative emotions did not exist within the Mother Organism. They were impractical and incomprehensible things to her. So even though joining with her had been painful—that was Godfrey's own fault because he resisted—it was now bliss.

He became a nova inside her, a raging cloud of supercharged dust that blew through the world, igniting things and being ignited, burning white-hot and traveling impossible distances through space and time. He breathed out searing mushroom clouds and screamed colors. The world was his and he devoured it bite by bite, laying waste to the works of man and destroying the scurrying masses with searing heat.

Then the world was empty.

There was nothing.

He seeded it with himself and watched the cooling clay remains of the human race blossoming into a new and better kind that grew over the rubble of the old and lifted caps like mushrooms to the stars above, bathing in the pure light of the twinkling jewels above.

And in the back of his head, one last reasonable shred of his brain knew one thing for sure: he was tripping his brains out.

43

Wetness.
Dripping.
Pain.
Numbness.

These were the things Chipney had been feeling for some time now as he swam in and out of consciousness. He wasn't sure when he was dreaming and when he was awake. But now as he concentrated, focused, forced his brain to the surface of the mire of confusion, he remembered. The light. The fresh air. Then falling into that pool of rushing water that threw him against rocks and stone walls and then vomited him onto a muddy flat of dripping water.

He was not alone.

He knew, in that tomblike blackness, there was another. He could hear the low, rumbling breathing. A clotted, congested sound of tubercular lungs sucking moist, thick air.

He tried to move, but could not.

There was no feeling beneath his waist, just a frightful rubbery emptiness. Paralyzed. Yes, he knew then with a manic, building hysteria that he was helpless.

But he was not alone.

The other moved towards him, pressed its fungous, soft bulk against him and he went mad at its touch, its pressure, its nearness...for its flesh felt like, if anything, the flesh of a mushroom, bloated and warm. Pendulous breasts brushed against his face and he knew it was a female. He could feel larval things squirming in those heavy teats.

His hand fumbled at his tac vest and pulled out a flare.

He had to see.

He had to drive her away.

He had to keep that horror off of him.

The flare ignited, and the brilliance made his eyes burn, but he saw what hovered over him, that swollen face with its bubbling growth of pink fungus, the flies lighting off it, the bones jutting from the fungous hide. It lacked eyes and a nose. It had only a shriveling puckered chasm like a blow hole that suckered open and closed.

This is what he saw in the light before she knocked the flare away with a huge, fleshy hand of clear, glistening tissue. The fingers were slats, purple and black veins like wires beneath the skin.

Then the light was gone.

He began to scream as she tended to him, licking him with a rough and narrow tongue, cleansing his wounds with her own secretions, picking parasites from his hair. She cooed at him with a weird, shrilling sound that set him to trembling.

He thought she was going to kill him, devour him.

But as her hair fell over him like rotting kelp and that oozing, puckered mouth found his own, he knew she wasn't going to hurt him.

And he was certain of it when she shoved something between his lips that she had plucked off her own body. He tried to spit out. But she wouldn't have it. She wanted him to eat. He didn't know what it was, but its texture was soft and repellent...then his tongue became aware of its delicate, almost nutty flavor and he found himself biting into it. The juice that filled his mouth was sweet, fermented, effervescent...and he squirmed as it filled his body with chemical fireworks.

She made a grunting, slobbering sound.

But he understood. "Yes," he said, everything inside him beginning to take flight. "It's...it's very good."

44

Kenney stumbled into an immense grotto that was like a great tube made of fungus. The water was patched with iridescent mold that shimmered brightly in hues of purple and indigo. It was a living tunnel of pink fungus, orange and yellow mounded growths, and bright red posts that grew up out of the water like deep sea smoker vents.

They were everywhere.

And they were moving.

The fungus draped from the ceiling and grew in sheer nets and fine filaments that flashed colors like fiber optic displays. Ropes and cables of it connected everything together in an intricate spiderweb mesh. He moved past things like immense nodding mushrooms whose caps were shiny and ruby-red above and bubblegum pink below. His flashlight beam was filled with multicolored spores that attached themselves to him, making him feel queasy and weak, then exhilarated and dreamy.

This is it, he told himself. *You have reached the epicenter. This is the womb of creation, the birth chamber; ground zero of this immense fungus-thing that has been gestating beneath the ground for centuries.*

As he passed through rising yellow grasses that were like spines, soft as pillow down, it all made no sense to him.

Why was this allowed?

Why wasn't he barred from this place?

Why wasn't he attacked or at least pushed back from this fragile wonderland ecosystem of birth? Why was he allowed to wander blindly here?

Because the thing wants you here. It wants you to see and feel its true nature.

That made no sense, yet it made all the sense in the world.

The growths he saw everywhere with such wild, rich, yet ordered profusion were all dripping with nectar that became a mist in the air that he breathed in and made him feel giddy. He could feel it on his face and in his hair, in his mouth and down his throat. Its taste was much like wine—sweet, fizzing, sour, its bouquet a rapture to the taste buds.

You're stoned. You're fucking stoned.

And that, he figured, was the key to it all, the very basis. No wonder those people of Clavitt Fields could not give up their wicked ways and blasphemies (as their contemporaries viewed it). They were addicted to the psychotropic secretions of the fungus. They were wasted on the shit. Even though contact with the subterranean fungi physically mutated them, making them more like funguses and slime molds than human beings, they still could not live without the tripping, hallucinogenic ecstasies of it.

It was addiction.

It was nothing more than fucking addiction.

There was no witch cult in Clavitt Fields, just a bunch of deluded proto-hippy 'shroom heads tripping their fucking minds out. Turn on, tune in, drop out, man. Dig it, baby!

He giggled as he imagined those staid, buttoned-up Puritan types tripping their fucking brains out. God, what a revelation it must have been! What freedom from the chains and bondage of their religion and repressive lives it must have offered! The fungus must have come down in that *piece of star* (as Elena Blasden called it) and then began to grow in the hollows beneath Clavitt Fields and what was now Bellac Road. It must have made contact with the townspeople and its chemical attraction could not be denied. For once tasted, it would have to be tasted again even if it meant you would become a crawling mutant horror.

Yes, that's exactly how it was.

The fungus had called him here because it wanted to teach him the true history of this region.

Kenney didn't really want it…but, then again, he really had no choice in the matter. The consciousness of the Mother organism was a colossal thing that crushed him. He became a receiver.

He saw Clavitt Fields as it was in the 18th Century.

He saw Preacher Clavitt show up. He was some kind of fanatical zealot who practiced an extreme form of the puritan faith. It was he and his congregation that originally began building the town, but as blood calls to blood, soon enough dozens of families traveled west to join them. By the time of the War of Independence there were several hundred people in the village. But even then it was a bad place. Stories made the rounds of things heard calling from the dark woods, strange sounds echoing up from the well Elena Blasden had mentioned. Clavitt's people were a fearful lot that did not dare venture out after dark and looked to the Bible for strength against the unknown. Clavitt himself called the area a "blighted, pestilential run of haunted forest and dark, brooding hollows that must be purified by the hand of the lord".

Then Corben arrived.

He went by no other name and was considered a sage of sorts, though local gossip had it he was a warlock that escaped persecution in Europe. He took control of the village from the old, infirm Clavitt. He was a learned man, well-versed in herb lore and folk remedy. Straight away, he began curing the sick and making fertile the fields. He fashioned talismans and amulets, good-luck charms and love philters for the heartbroken. And slowly, inexorably, he began to wean the townsfolk away from Christianity and into some older, pagan religion. A religion where ancient deities were worshipped in shadowy glens, where animal sacrifice was offered to ensure the harvest, where maidens adorned in flower petals were given bodily in orgiastic rites.

Those were the tales that the locals fervently believed.

The truth was that Corben was something of a 18th century Timothy Leary, a hallucinogen guru that had studied widely in the orient. His cures and potions often contained trace amounts of psilocybin which created feelings of euphoria, good fortune, and geniality amongst their users...and sometimes, unreasoning terror.

Somewhere during this period, the acid guru made contact with the Mother Organism and began to actively cultivate her spores which created mild to extreme hallucinogenic effects. It wasn't long before the entire town was involved and enslaved to her...and happily so.

Clavitt Fields became increasingly isolated. There was a great deal of speculation by outsiders concerning interbreeding and resultant insanity, physical and mental aberrations. Soon enough, none of the local villagers would go anywhere near Clavitt Fields. They spoke of witchcraft and Satanism, the black mass and human sacrifice. Even the unspeakable acts of cannibalism and necrophilia were mentioned, that some dark cult worshipped hideous gods in moon-washed groves and gave their first born to slake the appetites of these creatures. Outsiders were frightened, and many had seen the evidence of witching: failed crops, diseased livestock, and unnatural births among their own numbers. But these things were the result of contact with the Mother Organism and nothing else. All the above was nothing but superstitious fantasy and old wife's tales.

The inhabitants of Clavitt Fields were more than happy to stay on their own lands. They disassociated themselves from the outside world because they had all, in their own way, achieved a higher state of consciousness via the fungus.

But that was hardly acceptable to the town fathers of Trowden, who saw iniquity breeding on their doorstep. Three trusted and honorable men were given the task of making a pilgrimage to the shunned and evil hamlet of Clavitt Fields. No townsmen of Trowden had visited those redoubtable environs in some time. It was a sinister, witch-haunted borough, after all.

The three men were Dr. Blair, Mr. Bowden, and Mr. Peel.

Their mission was not of a military order, though they carried muskets and Bowden sported a brace of pistols and an old Naval cutlass sharpened to lethal perfection. Their mission was simply recognizance. Regardless, they expected trouble of the most "vile awfulness" as Peel put it. The most foul sort of tales were told of that accursed village, of course, things concerning obscene rites held upon May-Eve and Candlemas, and their judgment was more than a little clouded.

It was near to twilight when they picketed their horses in a thicket a few leagues from the village—this was Bowden's idea being a former cavalry officer. And it made good sense to the others, the rationale being that in the case of quick retreat their mares would stand ready.

Although evidently an agricultural community of sorts, they saw that the fields of Clavitt were mostly uncultivated and overgrown with briars, wild grasses, uprisings of creepers and an unwholesome umbrage that seemed to quiver though there was no discernable breeze. It was said that here were to be found splendid fields of buckwheat, rye, and Indian corn, but they saw only bramble thickets and alder bushes, and no livestock—nary a pig or guinea fowl or plow horse.

Clavitt Fields clung to a series of blighted hills that rose and fell and twisted like the convolutions of a serpent. It was hard for Blair and the others to believe it had stood less than a century, for what they beheld was a seemingly ancient, depraved uprising of rotting half-timbered houses and clustered tall buildings crouching beneath dark gabled roofs. They jutted from hilltop and dell, a crowded see-saw maze that leaned out over the cobbled and brickwork streets as if they would fall at any moment. So congested were these eldritch dwellings, Blair later noted, that the sullen windows of those above looked out over the crowded rooftops of those below. Had you but fallen from one of those high, sagging porches you would've landed on the neighbor's roof and rolled out into the narrow, claustrophobic streets.

In Kenney's mind, he could hear a voice speaking. It was clear and concise and he knew it was the voice of Dr. Blair reading from his own journals nearly two centuries before:

"How can I ever adequately convey how it felt walking into that shunned, godless village? Beneath those gnarled, twisted locust trees and misshapen elms? Would I say that the air was leaden, heavy even, thick as curdled cream and such as easy to breathe? Would I describe to you that high, noisome stink of dampness and putrefaction that seemed to visibly ooze from root cellars and gutters? Yes, perhaps, for such is true. Those high houses leered with grim secrets, shuttered and sunless, lathed in a breathing, sinister penumbra that set my flesh to crawling. As we walked those deserted, suffocating streets and weedy passages, we could hear sounds coming from behind warped doorways and planked windows. And, God, what sounds! Bleatings and snorting and gruntings akin to hogs rooting at a trough, but all with a weird, demented near-human timber to them. We wondered silently what abominations, what verminous hybrids could utter such sounds. We could feel eyes upon us and smell ghastly, fetid odors emanating from shadowy doorways. Never was I—and am not now—one given to supernatural elucidation, but I swear as God is my witness, that there hung a malignant pall over that accursed town, a noxious ether of spiritual contamination that made me shiver, made something in me beg to cry out! Yes, had it not been for my two stalwart and robust companions, I would have fled that decadent, hellish place and lost *myself most surely in those clutching, black woods and lunatic verdure."*

That was what the rambling voice of Dr. Blair said in a suitably dramatic and wordy fashion.

Before long, the villagers of Clavitt Fields began to show themselves.

Blair's voice droned on: "And what a debased, perverted assemblage of flesh they indeed were! Good Lord! A sub-human drollery! Wizened, skeletal things with peeling faces and deranged anatomies. Some hunchbacked, others missing limbs, still others—it seemed—with too many. Their eyes (and understand that some had none to speak of, merely fleshy depressions where eyes would sit in sane physiognomies) were glazed and sightless, while others sported orbs that were nearly luminous, the color of glaring autumn moons. Dressed in rags and nursing tumorous growths and leprous contusions, they shambled from the shadows to look at us. To gawk and leer.

"And laugh! For they were all laughing at us! A hideous conglomeration of morbid human mushrooms!

"And one man with colorless hair the texture of straw, slid forward and fixed us with a single saffron eye set in an exaggerated face of humps and ridges. 'Ye came, did ye? We knewed ye would!' he said, that cyclopean face swimming close to my own. 'Wait until sunset, he say'd! They'll come through the weald, he say'd! They'll be afeared of that which they find and what find them, he say'd! By my troth, he say'd, liken it to worse things! And here ye are, kind gentry, and welcome one and all! Good morrow to ye!'

"At which point—I can barely write of it, my hands trembles so—he opened his ragged, mildew-patched waistcoat and exposed the flesh of his chest which was set with pustules, tumorlike bulbs, and what appeared to be juicy pink toadstools growing in noxious, fertile clusters! They pulsed with life! Then...yes, I must write of it...he plucked one free by its stem and offered it to us.

"'Have a taste, would you, governor? Have a wee taste and a prosperous journey, eh?'

"He staggered away, giggling, chewing on the thing he offered me which I swear cried out as he bit into it. A dozen others followed him — a congregation of deformed, diseased, inbred mongrels laughing at some joke we dared not know. Some howled at the stars poking out above and others gibbered and still others wept and gnawed at their own fingers.

"These, then, were the children of Corben, the demonic savior of this degenerated and stigmatical flock.

"Despite my revulsion, being a medical man I began to put questions to the afflicted concerning the nature of their abnormalities and morbid afflictions, but I received naught, only laughter and bestial sounds in reply. Some pointed to the earth, others to the sky, and one woman whom lacked a mouth of all things, gestured madly towards the moon which was then beginning to arise over the latticed tree tops and was the color of fresh blood. A child pointed to a foreboding tangle of shadows that coiled in the alleyway between two crumbling buildings. She could not stop giggling.

"We continued on, undaunted. The villagers left us alone. They were — despite their numerous physical and mental derangements — a cheerful assemblage. Laughing and dancing and jumping for what seemed great joy. But joy of what?

"The town was a knotted profusion of cul-de-sacs and dead-end crevices pressed between high houses and tall, stone buildings with black, mullioned windows when there were any at all. It was an easy enough place to lose oneself. Particularly for me since I had never once walked — nor wanted to — those crumbling brick streets. I fear that the unwholesome tales whispered about that town were more than enough to keep me at arm's length, though I had resided in Trowden some two-and-seven years.

"Anon, we found what Silas Bowden assured us had once been a most prosperous tavern. We pushed through the rotting door and into the shadowy, umbered interior. Inside, the air was black and greasy, smudged with unpleasant odors as of tombs and crematoriums. An awful, vaporous reek of decay and slime and depravity. I found it necessary to suck air through staunchly-clenched teeth. A few withered and unappetizing specimens of the village waited at dusty tables or beneath the sullen, flickering glare of a whale-oil lamp. A man was crouched in the corner near the hearth. He held his face in his hands, continually moaning as if in some dire pain or suffering some irreparable loss. But as I watched him, by God, I saw...I swear I saw...something white and wet wriggling beneath those fingers. A barmaid turned and looked upon us, immediately secreting a hand into her besoiled apron—a hand that was gray and bloated as of a fungi. And of the others? Their faces were hideous things, lumpy and leprous, distortions nature had never intended in her wisdom. It was as if their faces were composed of bread dough, warm and pliable, elastic even, that had been stretched and pulled in the most repulsive fashion so that eyes were pushed up into the vicinity of foreheads and the corners of those horrid, gashed mouths often were slit into the cheekbones themselves.

"'Good sir,' Silas Bowden put to that thing behind the bartop. 'We seek an audience with Master Corben. Could you be good enough—'

"'Up those stairs yonder,' was all he would say.

"And up those stairs we went, our hearts heavy and our minds verging on madness. A black, reeking slime slicked the corridor above and it seemed that the woodwork had gone soft with some morbid decay. We knocked at the door at the end and...God, can I continue? Do I dare scrawl what it was that answered our beckoning? Do I describe that face that sent us fleeing? That livid creeping mask, bloated and eyeless, a festering contusion wherein crawled worming things and dripped with a gray, stinking slime? Or those fingers like viscid toadstools that reached out to us? Or that creeping fungous jelly that purported to be the body of a man?

"*Forspent and affrightened, we fled and ashamed I am not to admit of this. That town...that man...God in Heaven, how can any of this be? From whence comes this witchery?*"

Then the voice faded and Kenney stood there in that lush garden of growing things, the womb of the Mother Organism...and giggled. He ran his hands up and down mushroomlike stalks, fondling sacs and breathing bags of tissue web.

When Dr. Blair and company made their report to the town fathers of Trowden, the general consensus was that a curse had fallen over the region, that soon the pestilence of Clavitt Fields would contaminate Trowden, too.

The evidence continued to mount, the fathers said.

Clegg the blacksmith and his wife—after a delectable mushroom pie—were roasting apples in the hearth with their fine, fat children when the apples began to sizzle and became tiny, human heads with nightmarish faces that screamed and chanted. Livestock had been found in the fields—gutted, half-eaten, dismembered. Three children had disappeared...though, true, one was later found gleefully running along the top of the town wall. Several maidens were found dancing naked in the turnip fields and Farmer Crogan, him of sober habits, spent an entire afternoon counting window panes in apparent dementia. Crops were failing. Wells were corrupt—the water has gone to a red, shivering jelly (Preacher Tagley said the jelly whispered obscene things if one were to but listen). And the maiden Korth...dear Christ, it was said she laid with a boy from Clavitt Fields and the midwife Rogers had a seizure at the sight of the creature that fell from the girl's womb—an undulating thing like a human maggot.

"A pox on us all," said Dr. Blair. "Dear God, a pox on us all."

Something had to be done.

Incited by Pastor VanDeeden, a band of militiamen and privateers led by Silas Bowden assaulted the village of Clavitt Fields. In broad daylight they assembled. Two cannons were borrowed from nearby Fort McKinnis. And soon enough the quiet, sullen byways of the *accursed village were resounding with the reports of musketry and the booming of cannons. Houses were set afire. Buildings came down as cannon balls blew their walls to rubble. And everywhere, a deadly, hungering conflagration of flames and smoke and screeching, inhuman forms that went down under barrages of musket balls. Things howled and mewled behind those shuttered windows and white, pustulant hands clawed from cellar doorways. The town was raided, ravaged, and razed. When they left all that stood was a skeleton of what had brooded there before—chimneys and walls and foundations, smoldering timbers and sagging rooftops.*

This was what the Mother Organism wanted Kenney to know so that he would understand. Much of it—particularly Dr. Blair's report—were very subjective in nature. And as to how much was true and how much was the raving of men under the influence of hallucinogenic compounds, it was up to Kenney to decide.

There was no fucking witchcraft or dark gods worshipped at pagan altars in moonlit glens. That was all mad bullshit. The only thing out on Bellac Road was some kind of massive alien fungus that perpetuated itself by addicting other life forms to its hallucinogenic properties and then, and then—

And then Kenney didn't know. That was the secret the Mother Organism would not share with him and not because she was some scheming, conspiratorial thing, but because she truly thought—and her thinking was more along the lines of chemical transmission—it was obvious. In the final analysis, she was as fucking wrecked as her worshippers.

This was food for thought and he figured there was something there, something pertinent, but he was in no shape to partake of it because he was tripping himself.

I just wanna go roamin' in the gloamin' with a bonnie mushroom at my side.

Nightcrawlers

He started to giggle and things around him started getting peculiar—darkly, macabrely funny. Inside his head, it was loud and surreal and out of focus. He was a teenager again, getting stoned and reading H.P. Lovecraft, zoning out on cosmic horror and banned books and rotting little New England towns and the things that crawled in them…except that now he understood the nature of Yog Sothoth and Shub-Niggurath and even old Azazoth himself. Just subjective impressions and mushroom dreams of other worldly things as seen by minds absolutely blown on hallucinogens.

Even old Abdul Alhazred was probably nothing but a buttonhead.

He watched the mutants…maybe they'd always been there or maybe they just arrived. They passed by, completely oblivious to his presence. They had been killers before, savages that attacked without mercy…but that was only because they were defending what was theirs, the last shreds of human aggression and xenophobia expressing itself with tribal violence. Something that was amplified by the properties of the fungus. They were tripping themselves into an insane battle rage like Norse berserkers gobbling up fly-agaric before going into combat.

Now, completely under the influence of the Mother Organism they were docile. Not warriors but farmers. They carried sacks of human and animal remains and dumped them into the slimy water where they would continue to break down into rotting organic matter. It was like fertilizer for the Mother. Once they had done this, they ate her mushroomy growths.

They weren't ghouls, and they had never been ghouls.

The dead were for *her*. She fed off the rich nutrients of decomposition and they fed off her. In the end, they were nothing but servitors, caretakers and farmers. They took care of the Mother Organism and she took care of them.

Kenney knew that the bones they'd found in the field that started this whole mess hadn't been buried from above, but pushed up from below.

Things began to blur and lose consistency.

The fungus and its weird growths around him filled the grotto in vibrant, chromatic colors that made him cry out in pure rapture as he tripped amongst slender blossoms, pulsating seed pods, tuberous roots, and radiant membranes that became faces that laughed at him. The world was a whirling cosmos and he was drunk on it, stumbling deeper and deeper into the womb of life until—

Until he saw something that turned his joy into palpable fear that was a green river of plasma he drowned in.

Toadstools.

He was in a chamber of toadstools.

At least, that's what they seemed to be. They grew in wild abundance all around him, pink and translucent, not toadstools at all but fruiting bodies swollen with spores. It had taken the Mother Organism several centuries to come out of her semi-dormancy and to flower into full, fertile health, but her life cycle was endless. Now she was ready to spread her bounty onto the world of men.

Suddenly, Kenney felt the rage the mutants must have felt.

He saw a world of pulpous, inhuman servants tending to the needs of the Mother Organism. That was her plan. It was simple, natural, and non-violent. And to her it was perfection. She could not understand why anyone wouldn't want to be part of her. All life existed to be part of her.

She was not arrogant.

She was not domineering.

She was no monstrous alien invader.

Her ways were subtle. Once you smelled her perfume and touched her, you were smitten as any man was with a beautiful woman. She would let you touch her, teasing you with her fragrance and texture and perfect lines. Then you would want to kiss her and taste her and she would allow it. By then you were addicted to what she offered and there was no going back. Then you would enter her and she would absorb you, only to process you out as one of the mutants.

Then your life was cultivation.

Keeping her fertilized, adored, and well-stroked. Your reward was the pipe dreams she offered, the multi-dimensional trips through time and space. In the end, she was vain as any beautiful narcissistic woman who worshipped her own image in the mirror.

Bitch. Evil, inflated, egotistical bitch. You seduce us and addict us and make us into worker ants. That's why you came here. That was your agenda—to be what nature intended you to be, a planetary life form, a single vegetative entity.

It was all true and he knew it.

Yes, but a happy one. A happy, productive entity, she said in his head…though there didn't seem to be anything like a voice, just images and vibrations.

He stared out across the acres of her fruiting bodies. There were thousands and thousands and thousands of them.

He wanted to tear them up by the roots and squash them, charge through there with a scythe and reap them all, destroy them before they destroyed all that he knew…and yet part of him wanted to wear garlands of them and sing their praises to the world of stupid animals.

Feed your head, she told him.

In the end, he sat there chewing on a small mushroom and enjoying its taste, considering things like destiny and spatial perception and how this reality was like a film that could be peeled free when you achieved 100% consciousness through the offices of the Mother Organism.

Sneaky underhanded bitch, his last shred of free will thought. *You picked the right race, that's for sure. Nobody falls prey to addiction like we do and nobody enjoys getting trashed more than human beings.*

As she showed him alien vistas and networks of fluttering chromatic colors that he could smell and let him peek through long-shut doors of ultimate perception, he was reduced to some spastic delirium. It felt like his eyeballs were sweating, then bulging with hydrostatic pressure. His heart was not just racing, it had grown legs and it was kicking its way out of his chest. His skin was bubbling cheese, his mind a simmering broth, a sweet mushroom stew. When he cried out, his voice came not from his mouth but cycling out of the top of his head, leaving purple ripples in the air that refused to dissipate. When he reached out and touched them with fingers like spoons, they rang out like tuning forks.

Dream with me, she said in his head with a voice that was like the fluttering of a dozen butterfly wings. *There is a quiet path through the woods. Let me show you the way into the light…*

"Hee, hee," he giggled, swallowing the last bit of mushroom. "Lead on, fair lady…"

45

In a lonely, weathered farmhouse on Bellac Road, Elena Blasden was dying and in her mind she could see the faces of her children and hear their singing voices and it was a melody that would carry her higher up into the fields of the Lord. She was not frightened. At the edge of death, there is no fear. Emotions and anxieties which keep the human animal chained to the bedrock of its insecurities are cast off. As the eyes close, an inner eye opens briefly that sees all and understands and looks forward but never back. So Elena did not fear death because she saw the reality of it now in her dimming mind which was rooted to her fading body like a dead oak to soil leeched of nutrients.

She saw death not as a horrid Grim Reaper cutout taped to a Halloween window, but as a bandage that covers the wound that is known as life. The dying do not fear and the dead do not bleed.

Death had been coming for many hours now and as darkness took Bellac Road, holding it tightly and grimly in its fist as it always had, she remained slouched in her old rocker by the window, watching through eyes bleary with the years as the sun set for a final time in her life. It was beautiful and nothing could take its image from her.

Her bones were like a precarious structure of straw that held her together in one piece but would not hold her much longer. But by then, the true weight of Elena Blasden would be long gone, and she looked forward to the journey.

She heard a fumbling at the back door.

Was it them? Had the ones from below come for their feeding on this night when she could no longer offer them anything?

The idea that they might come in and feed on her made a girlish laughter erupt somewhere in her head. *Me? Me! Ha, a bag of withered sticks and threadbare jerky tough as pine bark! Let them come! Let them go away with indigestion and loose teeth!* The laughter echoed into nothingness and she remembered her girlhood and the precious, lost days of youth. She remembered what her mother had given birth to and how Midwife Sterns took it away into the night to be planted like a fat seed in Ezren Field. This was all she could think of.

The door?

Yes, it creaked open and hesitant footfalls came into the house along with a smell of dying things thrown up on dark beaches. *Shuffle-shuffle-shuffle*, came the feet, and she sensed rather than saw a crooked figure in the doorway. It breathed hard and things dropped from it.

She felt no fear.

"You've come then?" she said in a dry, cracking voice. "Is...is that you, Edwin? Is that you, Eddie?"

The footfalls came closer, and a shadow fell over her.

"Eddie," she said. "My dear brother...I'm so...tired...I'm so very tired..."

The figure scooped her up in its arms gently, and not without love, clutching her to him as she closed her eyes and vanished in the dreams of childhood that claimed her final moments.

The figure held her like a precious antiquity and took her away, down into the darkness where there was no pain and there was no fear.

46

They stood around the cistern staring down into the vaporous blackness.

They paced and muttered and swore and shook their heads.

Hyder stood there, staring, staring, watching the men around him out of the corners of his eyes, men who couldn't seem to stand still or didn't know what to do with their hands or where to put their eyes.

Finally, he said, "It's been four hours now. Somebody's got to go down after them and I guess that somebody is us."

"We shouldn't have waited this long," Snow said.

A few others grunted in agreement.

"The sheriff and I had an understanding," Hyder explained. "No one went down until the four hours elapsed. That's what he wanted. Those were his orders and I followed them."

A few of them looked like they wanted to argue the fact, especially the State Patrol cops—Kenney's people—but they never got the chance.

The ground beneath them made a curious grumbling noise. It rumbled again and this time the old farmhouse moved. They all felt it. Like something beneath it had stirred.

"Hell is that?" Snow said.

He was greeted by pale sweaty faces that had no answers at all.

The rumbling sound came again and was louder. This time it nearly knocked them off their feet like a subsurface seismic wave. The dirt floor of the cellar seemed to ripple. The cistern made a creaking sound and a few loose bricks fell down into the water below with muted splashes.

"Shit," Hyder said. "I think we're in a hell of a spot."

Understatement...because the rumbling made the house move this time like it had been shoved a few inches on its foundation. Then things really got going. The house shook and trembled, invisible waves of force passing beneath their feet. The mortaring of the bricks in the cistern crumbled and the entire thing began to collapse. The ancient flagstone walls shuddered, then made loud grinding sounds, and visible cracks like exaggerated lightning bolts fanned through them and they began to flake away.

As dust and wood splinters fell from above, Hyder grabbed one of the deputies and shoved him at the staircase which made a cracking sound loud as a pistol shot. Two of the steps snapped in half.

"Go! Go! Go!" Hyder cried. "Get upstairs! Get the hell out of here! Whole goddamn place is coming apart!"

How right he was.

There was a pained groaning from the house above them and the rough-hewn planks of the ceiling began to buckle. One of the timbers split lengthwise. It was like some colossal beast had the farmhouse in its grip and it was crushing it. The cistern completely collapsed into the hole below along with all of its bricks, taking a good section of the floor with it.

Hyder grabbed a state cop right before he would have gone tumbling down into the deep six below.

Then they were all climbing the rickety, shifting staircase that was beginning to break loose from its moorings. Something very heavy fell upstairs. They heard glass breaking, and it seemed like the house leaned to the side about three or four feet.

Hyder was the last one up.

He saw an entire section of flagstone wall crumble into rubble and part of the ceiling cave-in. The stairway shattered into kindling seconds after he got to the main floor.

Upstairs, the walls were breaking apart. The ceiling coming down. The corridor to the kitchen and outside was lopsided, the walls cracking open, the air filled with clouds of rolling plaster dust.

Hyder and the others just barely made it outside.

They stumbled through the wet grasses in time to see the farmhouse fall into itself with a great groaning death cry of ancient beams and straw-dry joists. Then it began to sink, falling into some widening chasm as if the earth was hungry and the wreckage of the house was a snack.

But even out in the field, there was no safety.

Not really.

In the brightness of the rising full moon, Hyder could see the crowds out there on the road, some of them newsies from the papers and TV stations who wanted to know how they'd managed to lose so many cops out here, but most just curious locals and people from nearby towns who thought something like this was a tourist attraction.

The earth tremor from below — or whatever the hell it was — had not subsided; it was still rolling and gaining momentum, if anything, like a wave preparing to crash onto a beach.

The ground was shaken like a rug and Hyder and the others kept falling on their asses and colliding with each other and getting tossed through the air. Out on the road there was shouting and horns beeping, cars smashing into one another and being backed right into the ditches. Pandemonium. And it seemed to be coming from every direction.

The other cops, all of them much younger than the undersheriff, were sprinting across the fields, falling, getting up, and running that much faster, leaving Hyder far behind. A shock wave came from below that threw him up in the air and with such force he flipped over twice before he came down with an impact that knocked the wind right out of him.

By then, all he could hear was the pained rumbling from below and the screaming of dozens of people.

As he climbed drunkenly to his feet, swaying and dizzy, he saw a great section of the field collapse in the moonlight as if a mammoth sinkhole was opening up. Even in the distance where the woods began, he saw stands of trees drop down into the earth as it yawned wide.

Then—

He saw something come rushing up from below like a surging tide of pink jelly, gushing and foaming, filling the chasm and overflowing it. There was another roaring eruption and a good part of Bellac Road simply vanished, taking dozens of cars and countless screaming, hysterical people down into the widening crevice. More of the jelly surged out, flooding over those that tried to run from it.

On his ass on a spit of somewhat stable ground, Hyder saw the various chasms widen and connect into a gigantic pit that stretched far into the forest—or where it had been—and to the road and beyond for several hundred yards. The seething pink jelly was like blood from a gashed artery spilling out and then it subsided as something rose from its depths, not one thing but many and for the life of him it looked like—

Mushrooms. Fucking mushrooms.

Yes, mushrooms and toadstools, but gigantic things the size of garages and two story houses, looming and rising, each of them painted in brilliant, vibrant oranges and yellows, greens and blues and electric purple. All phosphorescent, turning night to day. It made his eyes ache looking upon them. Some toadstools were narrow like morels and tall as oak trees, rising up like posts with distinctive and elaborately ridged caps. The mushrooms were smooth and saucer-shaped, bearing scarlet spots and swirling bands of brilliant color. Rising amongst them were immense domes—puffballs that seemed to be swelling like eggs ready to crack open. There were literally hundreds of these things, tall and short, oval and bloated, massive buttons sprouting in tangles and clusters.

A forest of writhing pink tendrils connected them in a delicate filagree, spreading out in webs, each of them branching out into a dozen or more fibers. The assemblage of fungi grew and grew, the ground shook and more of it fell away as new growths emerged, all of them rising up to the sky above, it seemed.

As it moved, rolled and undulated upwards, Hyder could see jagged cracks in the pulsating pale membrane that was its foundation, glimpses of something shockingly pink and writhing that seemed to be trying to break through.

He would have run, but there was nowhere to run to.

He was marooned on an island in a sea of germination.

In all directions, it seemed, was a malignant expanse of fungi that felled the forest and covered the land as it continued to expand. It brought a wet heat with it that steamed and smoldered, casting a drifting pall of mist over the world. It carried a stink of submerged things and organic decay.

Hyder still heard an occasional scream or a desperate voice crying out, but mostly there was silence, save for the occasional rumbling of the fungi and the rubbery sounds they made.

But everyone wasn't dead.

Where the road had been, there was still a piece of it left with a van and half a dozen people standing around it. They were in the shadows of toadstools that rose up to three stories or more now. They were staring up at them in awe and wonder, tendrils of mist wrapping around them.

Hyder heard a squishing sound, and a shape shambled out of the mist. It was a massive thing in the general shape of a man, but a man that had been bloated to obscene, impossible proportions, a man-like form that moved like a wave heading ashore. It was pulpy and distended and grotesque, a jellied mass of twitching, crawling things that hissed a yellow and venomous steam. A luminous shine came from it.

Hyder was not afraid.

He knew it was Kenney. He knew it was a friend.

He noticed then that every single cap was swelling now with nodules that were inflating like balloons until they must pop. Then they did like bubbles. But not exactly like bubbles. They exploded and cast vibrant clouds of yellow spores that spread out into a storm, a blizzard that was blown on the winds and settled back to the earth in a downy fall.

He stood up, raising his arms like a child greeting the first snowfall of winter and the spores settled over him, adhering to him. They were in his hair and covering his body. He tasted them on his tongue and breathed them in. Under their gentle caress, he settled back into the grass and dreamed beautiful, amazing things, his system overloaded with psychotropics that opened up febrile, impossible panoramas in every direction.

47

Later, he was still sitting there, content and happy, studying the spores that looked like pulsing blood blisters on the back of his hands. His body was swollen with their secretions, his legs now firmly rooted into the soil, strange tubular growths like ghost pipes rising up from him and spreading oval cups to take in the delicious moonlight.

He thought about Haymarket and Bellac Road, Kenney and the other cops. All that he had known was slipping away rapidly, and being replaced by a communal joy that was being of the body of the Mother Organism. The world at large would soon know the rapture that was his.

Brushing webbed fingers over his spongy lips, he recalled the reality he had once known with its petty greed, jealousy and meaningless competition. And as it faded into the fog of his mind, he heard the voice of his youth say, "It's all gone now. It was all just a bad trip."

Then he laid back, his multiform tendrils and shoots digging deeper into the dark, rich Wisconsin soil of his birth.

About the Author

Tim Curran is the author of the novels *Skin Medicine*, *Hive*, *Dead Sea*, *Resurrection*, *Hag Night*, *Skull Moon*, *The Devil Next Door*, *Doll Face*, *Afterburn*, *House of Skin*, and *Biohazard*. His short stories have been collected in *Bone Marrow Stew* and *Zombie Pulp*. His novellas include *The Underdwelling*, *The Corpse King*, *Puppet Graveyard*, *Worm*, and *Blackout*. His short stories have appeared in such magazines as *City Slab*, *Flesh&Blood*, *Book of Dark Wisdom*, and *Inhuman*, as well as anthologies such as *Shadows Over Main Street*, *Eulogies III*, and *October Dreams II*. His fiction has been translated into German, Japanese, Spanish, and Italian.

Find him on Facebook at:
https://www.facebook.com/tim.curran.77

Bibliography

<u>**Novels**</u>
Afterburn
Bad Girl in the Box
Biohazard
Blooding Night
Cannibal Corpse, m/c
Clownflesh
Dead Sea
Doll Face
Graveworm
Grim Riders
Grimweave
Hag Night
Hive

Hive 2: The Spawning
House of Skin
Long Black Coffin
Monstrosity
Nightcrawlers
Resurrection
Skin Medicine
Skull Moon
Terror Cell
The Devil Next Door

Novellas
Blackout
Corpse Rider
Deadlock
Fear Me
Headhunter
Leviathan
Puppet Graveyard
Sow
Tenebris
The Corpse King
The Underdwelling
Toxic Shadows
Worm

Collections
Alien Horrors
Bone Marrow Stew
The Brain Leeches and Other Eldritch Phenomena
Dead Sea Chronicles
Here There Be Monsters
Horrors of War
Zombie Pulp

Curious about other Crossroad Press books? Stop by our website: http://crossroadpress.com
We offer quality writing
in digital, audio, and print formats.

Subscribe to our newsletter on the website homepage and receive a free eBook.

Printed in France by Amazon
Brétigny-sur-Orge, FR

21009847R00140